Rachel Renée Russell

Double

DORK

diaries

First published as an omnibus edition in Great Britain in 2017 by Simon & Schuster UK Ltd
A CBS COMPANY

Simon & Schuster UK Ltd
1st Floor,
222 Gray's Inn Road,
London WC1X 8HB

Dork Diaries: TV Star first published in Great Britain in 2014 by Simon & Schuster UK Ltd, a CBS company.
Originally published in the USA in 2014 as Dork Diaries 7: Tales from a Not-So-Glam TV Star by Aladdin,
an imprint of Simon & Schuster Children's Publishing Division.

Dork Diaries: Once Upon a Dork first published in Great Britain in 2014 by Simon & Schuster UK Ltd,
a CBS company. Originally published in the USA in 2014 as Dork Diaries 8: Tales from a Not-So-Happily Ever After
by Aladdin, an imprint of Simon & Schuster Children's Publishing Division.

A CIP catalogue record for this book is available from the British Library.

ISBN 978-1-4711-6587-0

www.simonandschuster.co.uk
www.simonandschuster.com.au

SIMON AND SCHUSTER

Nikki's Reality Show Nightmare:
Lights... camera...
starring:
~~Nikki!~~
Mackenzie??
Uh-oh!

Is Nikki destined for TV stardom?! Or is it a step too far for Queen of the Dorks? Find out in *TV STAR*...

OMG!! I STILL can hardly believe what happened to me yesterday!! THREE totally-awesome-completely-unbelievable-too-good-to-be-true-exciting-wonderful things!!

Totally-awesome-completely-unbelievable-too-good-to-be-true-exciting-wonderful thing #1: I ACTUALLY WENT TO THE VALENTINE'S DAY SWEETHEART DANCE ☺!! SQUEEEE!

Yep! It was girls ask the guys! And at the very last moment, I FINALLY got up the nerve to ask my crush, Brandon!

Totally-awesome-completely-unbelievable-too-good-to-be-true-exciting-wonderful thing #2: I WAS CROWNED SWEETHEART PRINCESS ☺!! SQUEEEEEEEE!!

I still don't know exactly how THAT happened. But it did! And I have my TIARA to prove it!!

And finally, the most AMAZING thing EVER!

SQUEEEEEEEEEEEEE!!!

Totally-awesome-completely-unbelievable-too-good-to-be-true-exciting-wonderful thing #3: DURING THE VERY LAST DANCE OF THE MOST PERFECT, ROMANTIC, FAIRY-TALE EVENING, BRANDON AND I . . .

Hey! Wait a minute! Is that my cell phone ringing?!!

YES! My phone IS ringing!!!

Hey! Maybe it's . . .

BRANDON!! ☺!!!

(Checking my caller ID . . .)

NOPE!! It's NOT Brandon calling.

WAIT!! OMG!!! I can't believe it's . . .

He's just THE most famous TV producer in the entire WORLD! And the host of my FAVORITE TV show, a reality TV show/talent boot camp called . . .

4

15 Minutes of FAME

SQUEEEEEEE ☺!!

Gotta answer my phone!

I'm on spring break from school this entire week. So I'll have plenty of time to finish writing this . . .

LATER!!! ☺!

OMG! Saturday night was a complete NIGHTMARE!! How bad was it? SO bad I'm breaking into a cold sweat and having traumatic flashbacks just writing about it.

AAAAAAAAAAAAHHH! That was me screaming!! Sorry!! Must. Stop. Screaming! Anyway . . .

I can hardly believe the KA-RAY-ZEE mess I got myself into THIS time!

I wondered if they allowed diaries in JAIL! Because that's exactly where I was headed. No JOKE!! The authorities were about to place me under arrest ☹! But girlfriend wasn't going down without a fight!

And by fight, I mean trying to figure out whether I could sneak out of a nearby window, crawl onto a six-inch ledge, dangle by my fingertips over a railing, and then jump five floors to the ground below . . . without SPLATTERING myself all over the parking lot!!

Hmm . . . ?!

Probably . . . NOT ☹!!

But it gets worse! My BFFs, Chloe and Zoey, were getting arrested too. And it was all MY fault!

I was such a HORRIBLE person! I TOTALLY deserved it if they UNFRIENDED me on Facebook!

If only I HADN'T dragged them into this MESS!

I was just minding my own business and writing in my diary when I got that call Saturday morning. . . .

"Hello, Nikki! Great news! I'm in town today with my new group, the BAD BOYZ! I'd love to meet with you to discuss recording your band's song 'Dorks Rule!' The only problem is that we'll be leaving soon to go on a world tour. So I can only meet with you TONIGHT. Otherwise, it'll be about seven months before my schedule clears up again. Do you think you can make it to the Bad Boyz concert tonight?"

"OMG! Mr. Chase?! Yes, I'd love to! But that concert sold out months ago in, like, ten minutes. My two BFFs camped out in line overnight and STILL couldn't get any tickets."

"No problem! I'll give you three backstage passes so you can bring a couple of your band members. Just pick them up at the reserved—tickets window, okay?"

That was when I completely FAINTED! Well, actually, ALMOST completely fainted.

"Backstage passes?! That's AWESOME! Thank you, Mr. Chase! I'll see you TONIGHT!"

I could NOT believe this was happening! My band, Actually, I'm Not Really Sure Yet, might get a record deal! I hung up the phone and immediately called Chloe and Zoey to see if they wanted to go to the concert.

They answered with one word: "SQUEEEEE!" ☺!!

We all agreed it was going to be the MOST fun we'd had together since, um . . . yesterday!

When we arrived at the arena, we waited in line with THOUSANDS of excited fans. But you'd NEVER guess who we just happened to run into on our way to the ticket window. . . .

MACKENZIE ☹!!!

And of course she was surprised to see US, too!

"OMG! What are YOU losers doing here?" she said, turning up her nose at us in disgust like we were . . . a bunch of lowly . . . maggots . . . suffering from a terminal case of . . . diarrhea or something.

"We're here to see the show! What else?" I answered, like it wasn't a big deal at all.

"Well, have fun way up there in the cheap, nosebleed section. I managed to snag FRONT-ROW SEATS! If the Bad Boyz come down onto the main floor, I'll tell them you guys said hello. NOT!!" MacKenzie taunted.

Then she waved her tickets right under our noses really sloooowly like they were freshly baked red velvet cupcakes with extra sprinkles or something.

But I just stared right into her beady little eyes.

"Well, girlfriend! I hope you have fun in the front row, because WE'RE going to be BACKSTAGE!!" I said.

11

Then I waved OUR tickets right under HER nose really sloooooooooowly.

"Yeah!" Chloe added, doing jazz hands. "We have VIP, special access, BACKSTAGE PASSES! While WE meet and greet, YOU can weep!"

"And if WE run into the Bad Boyz backstage, we'll tell 'em YOU said hello," Zoey said, batting her eyes all sweetly. "NOT!!"

MacKenzie just stood there in shock, staring at us with her mouth dangling wide open.

The thought of us dorks hanging out with the celebs backstage must have given MacKenzie a mini nervous breakdown or something. Because she accidentally knocked over her bottled water and completely drenched Chloe!

Thank goodness Zoey had a pack of tissues in her purse.

We tried our best to calm Chloe down and dry her off.

CHLOE, FREAKING OUT AFTER
MACKENZIE SPILLED WATER ON HER!!

I couldn't believe MacKenzie didn't even bother to apologize to Chloe for being such a KLUTZ. She just disappeared. How RUDE!!

Anyway, since the show was going to be starting in less than ten minutes, we placed our coats and stuff in a locker and rushed to the backstage entrance. A grumpy-looking security guard was stationed there, checking IDs and buzzing people in.

"Um . . . excuse me, sir," I said excitedly. "We need to get backstage. We were invited here by Mr. Trevor Chase and have backstage passes."

"Yeah, right!" he grumbled. "And I'm Sleeping Beauty! You and nine hundred other girls ALL have backstage passes. Now, stop bugging me before I have you removed from the premises for attempted unauthorized entry!"

"No, we REALLY do!" I said, opening my purse to grab our tickets. "SEE? They're right here . . . !" Only there was a small complication. The tickets weren't in the little pocket thingy inside my purse.

14

"Um, wait a minute . . . !" I giggled nervously as I dug around in my purse. "I just have to find them. . . ."

The security guard rolled his eyes and glared at me.

"Nikki, give the nice man our tickets. Now!" Zoey said with a fake smile plastered across her face.

"Stop messing around before you get us thrown out of here," Chloe whisper-shouted in my ear.

I grinned at the scowling security guard. "Um, sir, could you please excuse us for a moment?"

We turned our backs to the security guard and huddled together for an emergency meeting. "I CAN'T FIND OUR TICKETS!!!" I shrieked quietly. "It's like they've disappeared into thin air."

"WHAT?!!" Chloe and Zoey both gasped.

"Maybe I just overlooked them . . . ," I muttered as I frantically dumped out my purse.

ME, DUMPING OUT MY PURSE WHILE TRYING TO FIND OUR LOST BACKSTAGE PASSES

But there were no tickets to be found. That's when we started to PANIC.

"Listen, they've got to be around here somewhere!" Zoey said, trying to stay calm. "Nikki, you rush back to the ticket window to see if you left them there. Chloe and I will check the locker to make sure you didn't leave them with our coats and stuff. Don't worry, guys. I'm SURE we'll find them!"

Then we took off in search of our lost backstage passes. By the time I made it back to the ticket window, it was closed because the show had already started. Unfortunately, I didn't see our tickets anywhere. And Chloe and Zoey didn't have any luck either.

It was my brilliant idea to call Trevor Chase and explain our predicament. But unfortunately, his voice mail was full ☹.

Things quickly went from bad to worse. When we told the security guard we'd lost our tickets and asked for his help, he just yelled at us.

"You have exactly sixty seconds to GET OUT of my arena!!" he snarled. "Or I'll place you all under arrest for TRESPASSING!!"

That's when I got really mad and totally lost it. "Yeah right, MR. GRUMPY! It's not like YOU actually own this arena. Besides, you're not even a REAL police officer!" I screamed at him.

But I just said that inside my head so no one else heard it but me.

I had a really SICK feeling in my stomach. Only one other person knew about our backstage passes.

MACKENZIE ☹!!

And now it was quite obvious to me that she had accidentally-on-purpose dumped water on Chloe to distract us, and then disappeared into thin air.

Right along with our TICKETS ☹!!!

OMG! I felt so angry and frustrated, I wanted to cry! If I didn't somehow figure out how to get backstage to see Trevor Chase ASAP, our record deal was going to be HISTORY!!

He MIGHT be available again in seven months. But life is SO uncertain. Hey, HE could be DEAD by then!! My BFFs were even more disappointed than I was.

"I'm really sorry things didn't work out as planned, Nikki!" Chloe said glumly.

"Yeah, what CRUDDY luck!" Zoey sighed.

We really didn't have any choice but to give up and leave. Plus, that security guard was eyeballing us like we were planning to rob a ticket window or something.

When he glanced at his watch, I knew he was probably thinking we only had thirty-five seconds left to get out of HIS arena or else!!

Heartbroken, Chloe, Zoey, and I blinked back our tears and then slowly began the long trek back to the front entrance.

My exciting career as a pop star has ended even before it officially got started.

Unfortunately, I have to stop writing now. My bratty sister and her crazy puppet friend, Miss Penelope, just came rolling up in my bedroom like they're my roomies or something.

Why was I not born an only child??!!

More later. . . .

☹!!

Now, where did I leave off yesterday?! Hmm . . .
Okay. My BFFs and I had just left the backstage
door area and were heading down the hall, when
the SCARIEST thing happened! We were almost run
over! By a rolling cart full of the most fabulous
designer stage clothing I'd ever seen in my life.
OMG! They were to DIE for!

I instantly recognized the famous fashion designer
Blaine Blackwell from that popular TV show, *Ugly
Dress Intervention!* and his new spin—off show,
Ugly Face Intervention!

He was talking on the phone a mile a minute! "Just
marvelous! Security is escorting me in. Your girls,
the Dance Divas, will be the best-dressed dancers
in the world . . . !"

Chloe, Zoey, and I stared at the rack of clothing
and then at each other. Without saying a word, we
knew exactly what we had to do. Together, we took
a running leap and dived in headfirst. . . .

CHLOE, ZOEY, AND I SNEAK
A RIDE BACKSTAGE!!!

After what seemed like forever, we cautiously climbed out of our hiding place. The clothes rack was sitting in a hallway right outside a door that said WARDROBE AND MAKEUP.

Our plan had worked! Chloe, Zoey, and I had actually made it backstage. Woo-hoo! We could hardly contain our excitement.

"Now we just have to find Trevor Chase!" I whisper-shouted.

"And avoid the security guards!" Zoey added.

"Yeah, this place is crawling with them!" Chloe said, and pointed to the far end of the long hallway.

Three guards were talking to Mr. Grumpy, the guy who'd told us to leave the premises.

That's when it occurred to me that security might be on the lookout for US! YIKES!! ☹!!

"Come on! Let's get out of here!" I muttered.

Suddenly, from right behind us, we heard a loud voice. "ACTUALLY, YOU GIRLS AREN'T GOING ANYWHERE!!"

OMG! The three of us peed our pants! Well, almost.

"FREEZE! Don't move a muscle! I'm about to SHOOT!"

We gasped, and clung to each other, TERRIFIED! I could NOT believe we were about to be GUNNED DOWN simply for sneaking backstage. That was so NOT fair!

"Just look at you! I really need to call the authorities and have you ARRESTED."

"P-please d-don't shoot! I c-can explain!" I stuttered. "I'm Nikki, and this is Chloe and Zoey. Mr. Trevor Chase asked us to—"

"I already KNOW who you girls are! Sorry, but I don't have a choice! Shooting people is my job! I'll try to make this as painless as possible. Now turn around, please, and face me!"

We gulped and turned around very slowly to see . . .

BLAINE BLACKWELL,
POINTING A CAMERA AT US?!

"Sorry, girls. But I always shoot a before and an after photo! If I were you, I'd be nervous too. Where do you ladies shop? The city DUMP?! Now, keep your eyes right on me. And say 'Cheese!'"

We breathed a collective sigh of relief!

"For a moment I thought YOU thought WE were, um . . . criminals!" I giggled nervously. "We're here to meet with Mr. Trevor Chase. He gave us—"

Blaine stepped closer to examine me and frowned.

"Honey, actually, those unruly eyebrows ARE criminal! And have you never heard of bronzer? It should be illegal NOT to use it. And that pukey orange sweater! You deserve the death penalty for wearing it in public! Have you no shame?!!"

I was speechless. OMG! Not everyone had the HONOR of getting ripped apart by the world-renowned Blaine Blackwell! Chloe, Zoey, and I just stared at him, totally mesmerized by his extreme awesomeness.

"Never fear, darlings! I've put together the most amazing wardrobe for your world tour! You'll be the three most FABULOUS, best-dressed dancers in the fashion-forward universe."

"But, but you're making a huge mistake!" I sputtered. "We're not backup—"

"No excuses, Miss Unibrow!" Blaine said, glaring at me. "Seriously! You ladies are a HOT MESS! Your makeovers are going to be a challenge even for me. Hey, I'm a world-famous designer and stylist, NOT a magician!"

"Did he just say MAKEOVERS?!" Chloe and Zoey squealed happily. "SQUEEEEEEE!"

We followed Blaine into the dressing room. Then he assigned each of us our very own hair, makeup, and wardrobe TEAM.

We also had our own vanity tables with lightbulb thingies around the mirror. And we got to wear the softest plush robes and slippers to lounge around in.

OMG, it was
A-MAY-ZING!

ME, ABOUT TO BE MADE OVER BY THE
FAMOUS BLAINE BLACKWELL!!

Chloe looked through the collection of lip glosses on
her vanity table. "Wow! I LOVE this pretty shade
of pink! I think it would look great on me."

As soon as she picked it up, Blaine rushed over to her.

"Honey, *NO!* Don't do it!!" he cried, and knocked the lip gloss tube out of her hand and onto the floor. "*OMG!* That was close!" he breathed heavily.

Chloe looked like she'd just seen a snake. "Was that lip gloss expired or something?!"

"Way worse than that!" Blaine gasped. "You were two seconds away from putting on a winter shade of lip gloss. And you are DEFINITELY an autumn!"

In less than an hour, I barely recognized my BFFs or my own image in the mirror.

OMG! We looked like a twist between fashion models and funky space aliens! Mostly due to our bright fluorescent-colored wigs and silver metallic glow-in-the-dark jumpsuits.

But one thing was for sure: I was TOTALLY convinced that Blaine Blackwell WAS in fact a MAGICIAN. . . .

OUR FAB MAKEOVERS, COURTESY OF BLAINE!

The best thing about our new costumes was that now we wouldn't be recognized by security.

Which was VERY convenient! Because according to the gossip in hair and wardrobe, a security alert had been issued by Mr. Grumpy (Gus the security guard).

Apparently, three teen girls had attempted to gain unauthorized entry backstage and then refused to leave the arena property after being instructed to do so by security.

They were now considered trespassers and were to be apprehended upon sight and physically removed from the premises.

Like, WHO does THAT?! Some girls my age are SO immature!

Anyway, the concert was going to be over in less than an hour, and the backstage area was huge.

But I was confident my BFFs and I would find Trevor Chase before it was too late.

I mean, how hard could it be?!

<u>JUST GREAT</u> ☹<u>! Now I have to stop writing in my</u>
<u>diary.</u>

WHY?!!!

<u>My mom wants me to take my little sister (Brianna</u>
<u>the Brat!) to the movie theater to see *Princess*</u>
<u>*Sugar Plum Goes to Hollywood: Part 2.*</u>

<u>UGH!! I HATE those stupid kiddie movies!!</u>

<u>I have this ENTIRE week off from school for</u>
<u>spring break. And I plan on spending it doing</u>
<u>REALLY SUPERimportant things like . . . um,</u>
<u>well . . . maybe writing in my diary and stuff!</u>

<u>Hey, it's NOT a vacay in Florida. But STILL!!</u>

<u>Sorry, Mom! But I refuse to spend all of my time</u>
<u>babysitting Brianna!!</u>

☹!!

Blaine Blackwell was right! Chloe, Zoey, and I were, without question, THE most FABULOUS, best-dressed dancers in the fashion-forward universe! Okay. Actually, THE most FABULOUS, best-dressed FAKE dancers in the fashion-forward universe!

We had just left hair and wardrobe when we heard an announcement over the PA system: "Trevor Chase, please report to the production office. Your limo to the airport is waiting."

"OH NO!" Zoey moaned.

"He CAN'T be leaving?!" Chloe groaned.

"We have to get to the production office!" I shouted. "Quick!"

I don't know how celebs and party girls do it. We could barely walk in our stiletto platform heels, let alone RUN in them!

"These stilettos are killing my feet!" Zoey whined.

"Well, you're lucky," Chloe grumbled. "I can't even feel MY feet. They went completely numb about two minutes ago!"

"Heads up! Three security guards straight ahead!" I whispered.

We tried our best to strut down the hallway like Glamazons. But our swaggers turned into crooked hobbles, which deteriorated into raggedy limps. It took FOREVER to finally reach the area where the production office was located.

"Yikes! More security!" I said under my breath.

As we passed them they eyed us suspiciously. Probably because we sashayed by like three clumsy horses in high heels. Clippity-clop, clippity-clop, clippity-clop!

But we just stared straight ahead like snooty, self-absorbed divas and ignored them. . . .

US, SASHAYING PAST THE SECURITY GUARDS!

I was SO relieved to see that the production office door was ONLY ten yards away. Then five, four, three, two . . .

My heart was pounding. Chloe and Zoey looked frantic. I placed my hand on the door handle, smiled, and whispered to my BFFs, "Thank goodness! We finally made—"

"STOP RIGHT THERE, YOUNG LADIES!" barked Mr. Grumpy as he quickly approached us.

"SORRY! NO AUTOGRAPHS!" Chloe practically screamed at him. "WILL SOMEONE PLEASE CALL SECURITY?! ON THIS . . . SECURITY?!"

I just rolled my eyes at that girl!

"I'm sorry to bother you girls," he said hesitantly. "But I just need to ask you an important question."

OMG! We were SO busted! We just held our breath and waited for the inevitable. . . .

"UM, DID SOMEONE JUST DROP THIS EARRING?
I FOUND IT ON THE FLOOR."

"Oh! I guess I did," Zoey said, relieved. "Thanks!"

"Since we're rich and famous celebs, those earrings probably cost ten dollars, I mean ten thousand dollars. All the cool Disney stars wear them too. We actually hang out with them," Chloe lied. "And tonight we're going to a party given by— OW! THAT HURT!!"

Thankfully, Zoey kicked Chloe in the shin to shut her up before she completely blew our cover.

"Come on, girls!" I said, plastering a fake smile across my face. "We have to get to that important meeting with Mr. Trevor Chase ASAP!"

"Have a nice evening," the guard said, nodding.

I couldn't believe we'd FINALLY made it! I was going to be SO happy to see Trevor Chase.

We opened the door and excitedly rushed inside. Then we stopped dead in our tracks and just stared in shock and disbelief. Because standing right there in front of us were . . .

NIKKI, CHLOE, AND ZOEY?!!

Well, that's what their ID badges said, anyway!

ARGH! I have to stop writing AGAIN!!

My dad just asked me to go to the mall with him to help pick out a birthday present for my mom. Her birthday is on Saturday, March 15.

Hey, people! I'm on SPRING BREAK!!

But you wouldn't think so with all of the demands Mom, Dad, and Brianna are placing on MY precious time off from school.

How am I supposed to write in my diary with all of these random INTERRUPTIONS??!!!

Anyway, more DIRT on MacKenzie tomorrow . . . !!!

☺!!

OMG! I could NOT believe MacKenzie and her friends Jessica and Jennifer were actually pretending to be US?! I mean, WHO does that?!!

It was bad enough that they'd stolen our tickets behind our BACKS. But now they'd stolen our identities right in front of our FACES!

Although, considering the fact that we'd just gotten makeovers AND were wearing fancy stage costumes AND were kind of pretending to be the Dance Divas, I guess you could say that maybe it WASN'T exactly in front of OUR FACES.

But STILL!! I was SO mad I could just . . . SPIT!!

That's when MacKenzie and her friends squealed and rushed right over to us.

"OMG! I can't believe you're actually the Dance Divas!! I'm Nikki, and these are my friends Chloe and Zoey!" she lied. "Could I have your autographs?

Please? Just write 'To MacKenzie: beautiful and brainy! A future pop star!' and I'll give it to her!"

Then she handed me a pen and paper.

"Nice to meet you, Nikki!" I said, playing along. "I'd love to give you my autograph. And I have a really inspiring message especially for you. . . ."

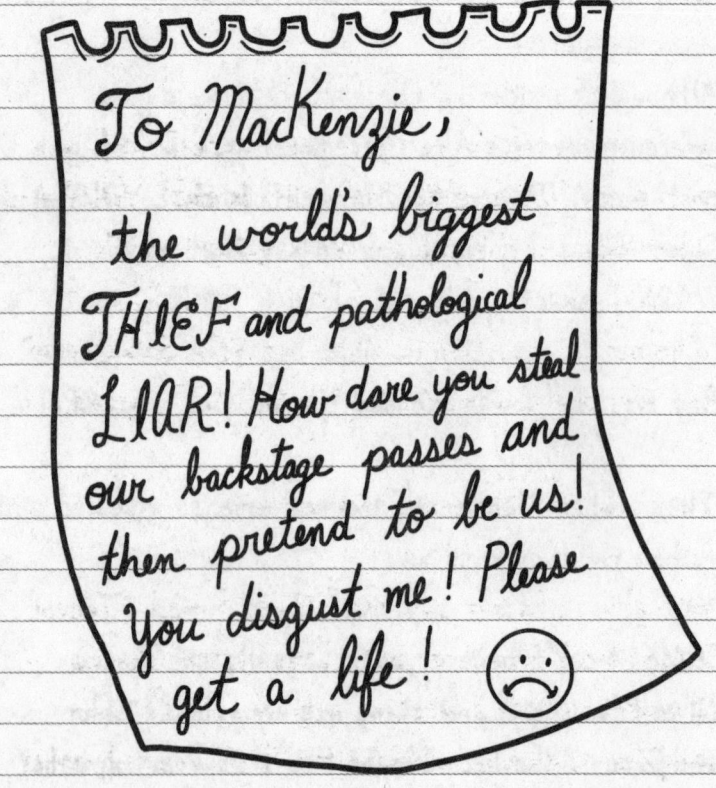

To MacKenzie,

the world's biggest THIEF and pathological LIAR! How dare you steal our backstage passes and then pretend to be us! You disgust me! Please get a life!

"Oh, thank you!" MacKenzie/Fake Nikki gushed. "I really appreciate you doing this for my good friend MacKenzie!"

Then, smiling, she dramatically read aloud what I'd written. "'To MacKenzie, the world's biggest THIEF and pathological LIAR' . . . ??!! WHAT?!!"

Suddenly she frowned and narrowed her eyes at me in an icy glare.

"Wait a minute! You're NOT the Dance Divas!" she sputtered. "OMG! Nikki Maxwell?! Is that YOU? And Chloe and Zoey! What are YOU doing here?"

"The better question is, what are YOU doing here? And why are you pretending to be US?" I asked.

"None of your business!" Jessica said.

"Actually, it IS our business!" Zoey fumed. "Trevor Chase gave Nikki those backstage passes! She was supposed to have a meeting with him. Until some lip-gloss-addicted, wannabe BANDIT dumped water on Chloe to distract us and then ran off with our tickets."

"Well, Nikki, too bad for you! I heard he just left for the airport." MacKenzie sneered.

My heart dropped right into my ~~shoes~~ stilettos! I couldn't believe we had gone through all of this drama and Trevor Chase had left without talking to us about our record deal.

I swallowed the huge lump in my throat and blinked back my tears. The last thing I needed right then was gooey black Glitter-Glam mascara streaming down my face.

"Yeah! So you guys can go CRAWL back under your rock!" Jennifer snarled.

Suddenly the door burst open and three security guards rushed in, led by Mr. Grumpy.

"What's all the commotion, young ladies?! We heard

44

your voices all the way down the hall! Is everything okay?"

"Actually, not!" MacKenzie spat. "These girls don't belong here. They're . . . IMPOSTORS!"

"What?! Are y-you sure?!" he stuttered.

The security guards stared at Chloe, Zoey, and me with really confused looks on their faces.

I was like, Oh. No. She. DIDN'T!! We were SO BUSTED! AGAIN!! MacKenzie was always sticking her nose in MY business.

Well, TWO could play this little game!! She STARTED it, but I was going to FINISH it.

"Actually, THEY don't belong here! THEY'RE the IMPOSTORS!!" I announced.

That's when the guards turned and stared at MacKenzie, Jessica, and Jennifer.

Those girls were squirming like slimy little worms on a hot sidewalk.

"Don't believe HER! They're NOT really the Dance Divas!" MacKenzie snarled.

"And they're NOT really Nikki, Chloe, and Zoey!" I shot back. "They stole OUR backstage passes."

Now the security guards were TOTALLY confused.

They just kept staring at me (the real Nikki and fake Dance Diva) and then the fake Nikki (really MacKenzie) and then back at me (the real Nikki and fake Dance Diva) and then the fake Nikki (really MacKenzie).

All of this staring went on, like, FOREVER! I have to admit, even I was starting to get a little confused about who was actually who.

"Nikki! You're lying!"

"MacKenzie! YOU'RE lying!"

Then we both angrily pointed at each other and screamed . . .

Then things got even MORE confusing! Three girls in dance leotards stormed in with Blaine Blackwell. They did NOT look like happy campers.

Blaine marched over, pointed his finger right in our faces, and screamed . . .

I guess Mr. Grumpy had heard enough! Because he glared at all of us with his eyes almost bulging out of his head. "US" being me, Chloe, Zoey, Jessica, Jennifer, AND MacKenzie.

Then he yelled at the top of his lungs like a lunatic . . .

"WHAT?!!!" we all gasped in SHOCK.

Everyone started talking at once!! Jessica and Jennifer burst into spontaneous tears!

The security guard continued. "Now, everybody just calm down! I don't have a choice but to detain ALL of you girls until we can sort this out!"

"Please, sir! Could you just let me explain?" I pleaded.

"Yes, I'll take all of your statements AFTER I file an initial report with the chief of security. But first, I'll have to call your parents—"

"OUR PARENTS?!!!" we all gasped.

"Just take a seat and make yourselves comfortable. I have a feeling it's going to be a long night. Now, do you have any questions?"

It was so quiet in that room, you could hear a pin drop.

I cleared my throat and then raised my hand.

"Yes, young lady, what's your question?"

"Um . . . c-could I go to . . . the b-bathroom?"
I muttered.

That's when I rushed to the bathroom and started
panicking that I was going to be sent straight to jail.

And praying that IF I actually went to JAIL,
they'd at least let me take my diary.

Then I had the most HORRIFIC thought!

WHAT if MacKenzie and I are forced to be
CELLMATES?!

I'd be STUCK serving a ten-year prison sentence in
a teeny-tiny cell with HER on the top bunk!

Just the thought of it made me break into a cold
sweat.

ME AND MY CELLMATE, MACKENZIE

Hey, it could happen!

AAAAAAHHH ☹!!

(That was me screaming!)

Although, I could always hire one of those famous criminal defense attorneys to appeal my case! And then I could try to convince the court to give me the DEATH PENALTY instead of a bunk with MacKenzie!

Hey, they could actually rule in my favor!

WOO-HOO!
☺!!

(I know, I know! I've been writing about what happened to me last Saturday night at that concert, like, FOREVER! Well, for at least four days now. Hey, maybe I'll make *Guinness World Records!* To be continued tomorrow. . . .)

THURSDAY, MARCH 6

This was the moment I'd been DREADING!

The chief of security was about to make the very first call to parents. MINE! Why ME? ☹️!!!

Probably because MacKenzie had convinced everyone that her parents were on a six-month-long hiking trip in the rain forests of Peru and the cell phone reception there was pretty much nonexistent.

That girl is SUCH a liar.

I mean, what IDIOT would even believe such a wacky story?! How about the ENTIRE security team?!!

They decided to take MacKenzie's suggestion and send a note to HER parents by carrier pigeon.

I just knew MY parents were going to KILL me.

But I tried to look on the bright side.

When they were found guilty of attempted murder, we could all go to prison as one big HAPPY family ☺!! . . .

OUR PRISON FAMILY PHOTO

And with me, Mom, and Dad out of the way, Brianna would have unlimited use of my CELL PHONE and get to eat her favorite meal—a big bowl of ketchup, raisins, and ice cream—for breakfast, lunch, and dinner. . . .

BRIANNA, HOME ALONE, GETTING STICKY
CRUD ALL OVER MY PHONE ☹!!

Just as I was about to give up HOPE (and my
parents' telephone number!), in walked the VERY
last person I expected to see.

No! It wasn't SANTA CLAUS, silly! It was . . .

TREVOR CHASE ☺!!

And everyone in the room immediately rushed over and started talking to him all at the same time, including ME!

"Trevor! I was tricked into doing hair, makeup, and styling for three common criminals. My Ugly Intervention reputation will be RUINED!"

"Our identities have been stolen by some Dance Divas wannabes!"

"Yeah, and they're not even very good dancers!"

"Dancers?! They can barely walk! You should have seen them staggering around here in those heels."

"Sir, we've apprehended six suspects in connection with a crime spree committed on the arena premises, and our investigation is ongoing."

"I'm MacKenzie! Remember ME?! I won the Westchester Country Day Middle School talent show with my amazing dance routine. Anyway, don't believe anything Nikki Maxwell is going to say about me. She's delusional because she forgot to take her meds today."

"Actually, YOU need help, MacKenzie! How dare you say such mean things about my BFF, Nikki, and 'whisper insidious accusations in the ear of the mob!'—Virgil."

"Hi, I'm Jessica, and I can play 'Yankee Doodle Dandy' on the accordion while tap dancing in pink designer cowboy boots. I'd be just perfect for your show! Listen to this. . . . 'Yankee Doodle went to town, riding on a po-neeee!'"

"Nikki is my BFF! So just back off! By the way, is anyone going to eat these cupcakes? Or these cookies? Or these brownies? Or these— OW! That hurt!"

"I just wanna go hooooome! Waaahhhhhh!"

"Sir, if you could just sign here, my security team will have the authority to press charges against everyone involved."

Finally Mr. Chase had had enough. "QUIET! Everyone! Please," he shouted. Then he continued. "Okay, I have just one very important question. WHO is responsible for all this RUCKUS?"

That's when ALL the very angry people in the room suddenly pointed at ME. . . .

ME, GETTING BLAMED BY A RUTHLESS MOB

The whole thing WAS my fault. Kind of!

If I'd just stayed home and shared a big bowl of ketchup, raisins, and ice cream with Brianna, NONE of this would have happened.

I stared at my feet and sighed. I was pretty sure I had kissed that record deal good-bye.

"Mr. Chase, I'm really, truly sorry about the mix-up. But our backstage passes went missing. So we had to kind of sneak backstage and then borrow the Dance Divas' costumes so no one would recognize us. And by the time we finally got here to talk to you about our recording deal, you'd already left. And then we got . . . ARRESTED! I'm really sorry I misled everyone and pretty much ruined your evening!"

That's when Trevor Chase stared at me with this perplexed look on his face.

"Do I know you? Wait a minute! Are you NIKKI MAXWELL?!" he asked, squinting at me closely.

First he smiled. Then he chuckled. Then he laughed. Hysterically, like he was losing his mind.

And soon everyone else in the room had joined in the laughter too.

Even ME! Although I didn't have the slightest idea what was SO darn funny.

"Blaine! You're a genius!" Trevor sputtered. "I was totally convinced Nikki and her friends were really the Dance Divas. I'd like to offer you a job doing hair, makeup, and wardrobe for my TV show!"

"I'd LOVE to!" Blaine gushed. "When I saw these three girls and their tacky clothing, unruly split ends, and that hideous unibrow, I felt so sorry for them. So I begged them to let ME do a makeover! Then I insisted on dressing them in my latest fab fashions. As I always say, I'm a stylist AND a magician!"

"So do you STILL want to press charges against them?" Mr. Grumpy asked, impatiently tapping his pen on his notepad.

"Press charges against them? Why, NO! The only thing criminal about these girls is the way they're murdering those stilettos. OMG! They walk like dizzy giraffes with jellyfish ankles."

63

I could NOT believe we were being ripped apart by the world-famous Blaine Blackwell, of Ugly Intervention fame. AGAIN! He made us feel like uncivilized barnyard animals. SQUEEEEEE ☺!!

"CASE CLOSED!" Mr. Grumpy announced. "And now that I've worked up an appetite, I'll just help myself to a few of these delicious pastries and then be on my way."

Thank goodness everything worked out so well in the end.

MacKenzie even apologized for "accidentally" stealing my tickets. She said she had been on her way to the bathroom, but somehow she'd gotten lost and ended up backstage . . . eating cupcakes while wearing an ID tag with MY name on it ☹!

Like, WHO does THAT?!! That girl is such a PATHOLOGICAL LIAR!

I think she started acting SUPERnice and sweet just to try to impress Mr. Chase.

And YES! After Zoey put me on a total guilt trip, I accepted MacKenzie's apology and decided NOT to press charges against her and send her to jail.

But that was ONLY because I felt REALLY sorry for the poor prison inmate who was going to get stuck sharing a bunk with her. Hey, I wouldn't wish MacKenzie on my worst enemy. Which, unfortunately, she IS ☹!

Anyway, Blaine let us keep our Dance Divas outfits, which inspired a brilliant idea for Halloween. We could paint our faces vomit green and be the Dead Dance Diva zombie queens. Am I not a GENIUS?!!

So we FINALLY had that meeting with Mr. Chase! And get THIS!! He said he was ready to move forward with recording our song "DORKS RULE!"

SQUEEEEEEE!

We'll be working with his producer at a local studio while he finishes the world tour with the Bad Boyz. He even decided to stay in town an extra day to launch a brand-new project.

Mr. Chase planned to meet with our parents to have them sign permission forms and contracts that following day, on Sunday. And afterward, he was going to treat all my band members to a pizza lunch at Queasy Cheesy and make a big surprise announcement!

Chloe and Zoey were SO happy! They said recording

a song was going to be the MOST exciting thing that had ever happened to them. They also told me I was a really wonderful friend! Even though I had almost gotten them arrested.

Then they both gave me a big GLAMAZON hug!

CHLOE AND ZOEY, SQUISHING
ME IN A BIG HUG

I was really looking forward to spending time with Chloe and Zoey in the studio.

And since BRANDON is our drummer, that meant I was also going to be spending a lot of extra time with HIM, too.

SQUEEEEEE!!

Although, I have to admit, deep down inside I am a little nervous about this project.

I have to remind myself it is just a song!

Not BRAIN surgery!

I mean, how hard can it be?!!!

☺!!

Gotta stop writing now! My mom is calling me for dinner. I'll finish writing about what happened next tomorrow. Hopefully!

I woke up Sunday morning feeling dazed and confused.

Everything that had happened Saturday night felt like a VERY weird dream.

Suddenly my cell phone rang.

Very loudly. . . .

DEET-DEET DEEEEEET! DEET-DEET DEEEEEET!

I covered my head with my pillow and groaned. But it kept on ringing. . . .

DEET-DEET DEEEEEET! DEET-DEET DEEEEEET!

Most. Annoying. Sound. EVER! Still groggy, I finally sat up in bed and answered it. . . .

It was my BFFs, Chloe and Zoey!

They were giving me a wake-up call and reminding me that we had a VERY important appointment at noon.

That's when I finally realized all of that CRAZY stuff had ACTUALLY happened to me!

Including the very COOL part about a record deal!

SQUEEE!!!
...

I quickly jumped out of bed and called Brandon, Marcus, Theo, and Violet to tell them the exciting news. Trevor Chase wanted to meet with all of us at Queasy Cheesy to discuss recording our song!!

When everyone arrived at the restaurant, Trevor had a short meeting with all of our parents and guardians.

Then he had a meeting with US kids. . . .

ME AND MY BAND, MEETING WITH
TREVOR CHASE AT QUEASY CHEESY

He explained that we would be recording with his
assistant producer, Scott, starting March 17 for
about two weeks.

Then, if all went as planned, our song would be released in June! SQUEEEEE ☺!!

Mr. Chase then announced that our band would be opening for the Bad Boyz at their next concert stop in our city!

Of course, all of us girls started screaming hysterically when we heard THAT news! And the guys all gave each other high fives.

Our listening party (yes, PARTY ☺!) was going to be held at the fabulous Swanky Hill Ski Resort on Saturday, March 29! And all proceeds from our CD sales at the party were going to Kidz Rockin', a charity that provides music lessons and scholarships to children. How COOL is THAT?!

Then Trevor smiled really big and announced that he was saving the BIGGEST surprise for last. OMG! I didn't think there could be any better news than all of the stuff he'd just told us.

Until he pointed at me said . . .

And get this!

A guy was standing there holding cue cards with stuff written on them that Trevor Chase was supposed to say on camera.

I just sat there blinking nervously with this stupid smile plastered across my face.

Then an entire television crew just appeared out of thin air.

A huge camera was pointed at me, a bright light flashed on overhead, and a microphone was stuck right in my face.

If I hadn't already been sitting down, I would have keeled right over.

My BFFs would have had to literally PEEL me off the floor.

Everyone at the table just stared in shock with their eyes as wide as saucers and their mouths hanging open.

I just sat there blinking nervously with this stupid smile plastered across my face. Then a huge camera zoomed in so close, everyone could probably see my nose hairs. . . .

Trevor then explained to our TV audience (TV AUDIENCE?!!) that a camera crew from our local TV station affiliate would start filming me on

Monday, March 10, and through the end of the month—at school, at home, practicing with my band, recording at the studio, and just hanging out with my friends and having fun.

I knew I was lucky to have such a wonderful opportunity. Hey, most kids would KILL to be in my shoes! Having a reality show chronicling my experiences as a POP STAR and ACTRESS was just so . . . I don't know . . . um . . .

GLAMOROUS ☺!!

But in spite of all of that, there was one tiny thing that TOTALLY freaked me out.

Namely, the possibility that a TV camera might be following me . . . .

HOME ☹!!

This could create a problem because I have a big secret. I attend my school on a bug extermination scholarship ☹!

And the bug exterminator has a raggedy van with a hideous five-foot-long plastic roach named Max on top of it. Unfortunately, all THREE of them live at my house ☹!

I swear! I will DIE of EMBARRASSMENT if the kids at my school see all of this SUPERpersonal stuff about my life on TV.

"So, Nikki!" Trevor read from a cue card. "What's your answer? Are you willing to let all of our viewers at home join you on this fabulous adventure in your quest for fame, by allowing them a peek into your very private life?"

That's when I noticed that all of my friends were staring at me, nervously waiting for my answer.

There was a very good chance this show could RUIN my life. I sighed deeply and bit my lip.

"Um . . . OKAY!" I answered as I looked directly into the camera and dazzled viewers with my bright smile and ADORKABLE charm.

But another part of me—a darker, more insecure side—wanted to scream my REAL answer to the WORLD at the top of my lungs. . . .

OMG! I'm going to be CRAZY BUSY for the next three weeks. My schedule is RIDONKULOUS!! Which is, like, ten times worse than ridiculous!

Filming TV show	Mon.–Fri.	8 a.m.–3 p.m.
Voice lessons	Mon.–Fri.	5 p.m.–6 p.m.
Recording sessions	Mon.–Fri.	7 p.m.–8:30 p.m.
Band practice	TBD	

I STILL can't believe I'm actually going to be recording my song AND filming a TV show! ALL at the same time! And on Monday, my first day back at school, I start practice sessions with my voice coach.

I just hope I'm not too busy to spend time with Brandon. I felt a little weird seeing him at Trevor Chase's pizza party. It was the first time we'd seen each other since the Sweetheart Dance AND . . . well, you know!

We both couldn't stop blushing, and I had a terminal

case of the giggles. But I really wanted to know how he felt about . . . um, the whole thing.

So I took a deep breath and just kind of blurted out my question while we were eating pizza. . . .

SO, BRANDON? ABOUT THE SWEETHEART DANCE. HOW DID YOU FEEL ABOUT . . .

But, unfortunately, things suddenly got SUPER
awkward. . . .

I felt too embarrassed to ask him with that TV camera around, so I totally chickened out.

I guess you're supposed to discuss really personal stuff like that in private. NOT at a pizza party with Trevor Chase, your FIVE best friends, AND a TV crew.

On TELEVISION!!!!

OMG! How EMBARRASSING would THAT be?!

I just hope none of the crazy stuff that's happened lately will change our friendship.

Because I think I might like him even MORE!

But get THIS. . . .

Before we left, he told me he had something really important he wanted to ask me. But he'd wanted to wait until we had a little more privacy.

I was really surprised to hear THAT news!

And now my curiosity is KILLING me.

I don't have the slightest idea what it could be.

Unless he wants to ask ME exactly what I was going to ask HIM.

SQUEEEEE!!

This GUY STUFF is so complicated.

And FUN!!

☺!!

JUST GREAT ☹!!

I think my mom is downstairs fixing a fancy Sunday dinner. Lately she's been watching all of those Food Network cooking shows, and now she's obsessed with the healthy cooking kick.

But the sad thing is that her cooking was never that good to begin with.

It's gone from VERY BAD to HORRIBLE!

Sorry, Mom ☹!

Probably the worst thing about her new meals is the very strong and pungent SMELL.

We had homemade pizza almost a week ago, and I STILL can't get the stench out of my hair.

And I've washed it THREE times.

Come on! HOW do you screw up a PIZZA?!! All you have to do is call the pizza delivery service, place your order, open the front door when you hear the doorbell, and THEN open the pizza box and eat it!!

Well, Mom got really creative and made a black bean crust pizza with chicken gizzard, okra, and beet toppings! And NO CHEESE!!!

Like, WHO does that?!!

It looked like roadkill, and tasted like it too!! But the WORST part was that it SMELLED like roadkill!

We needed, like, seventeen of those air-freshener thingies that you see in those silly television commercials. You know, the ones where they take two people and blindfold them and place them in a really foul-smelling, nasty place.

However, because they have an air-freshener thingy in the room, the people always insist they smell a spring flower garden with a hint of lavender. . . .

UNSUSPECTING COUPLE, THINKING
THEY'RE IN A CLEAN, NICE-SMELLING PLACE

But after they take off their blindfolds, they're
always SHOCKED and SURPRISED. . . .

UNSUSPECTING COUPLE, IN SHOCK
AFTER THEY REALIZE THEY'RE
SITTING ON A COUCH IN A PILE OF
MANURE, IN A FLY-INFESTED BARN,
NEXT TO TWO SMELLY COWS!!

ICK!!! ☹!!

Now that I think about it, maybe I'll just make a peanut butter and jelly sandwich for dinner.

SORRY, MOM!

☺!!

Today everyone was really excited to be back at school after our weeklong spring break.

Some kids vacationed in Florida. But ME? I mostly just hung around the house and wrote in my diary. Hey, I was just happy I DIDN'T spend spring break in JAIL! I still can't believe MacKenzie almost got all of us arrested like that!

I think her lip gloss addiction is FINALLY starting to affect her brain. Ever since that big fiasco at the Sweetheart Dance, that girl has been acting SUPERevil.

It wasn't MY fault she ended up in that smelly Dumpster in her expensive designer dress. Okay, so maybe it WAS my fault. A little.

But STILL!! She TOTALLY deserved it!

This morning I was at my locker, minding my own business, when she smiled at me and said . . .

That girl HATES MY GUTS ☹!

Calling MacKenzie a mean girl is an understatement. She's a cobra with hoop earrings, blond hair extensions, and a spray-on tan.

I glared at her. "Well, MacKenzie, YOU'RE the expert on toilets! It's only 8:00 a.m. and your BRAIN is completely CONSTIPATED while your MOUTH has a severe case of DIARRHEA! Please, go FLUSH!"

That's when she narrowed her eyes and got all up in my face like a hot double-cheese, pepperoni pizza. "You don't belong here, Maxwell! You're just a pathetic little FAKE, and I'm going to expose the truth to the entire WORLD! So you better watch your back!"

Then she cackled like a witch and sashayed away. I just HATE it when MacKenzie sashays. But I didn't have time to be worried about an immature, self-absorbed drama queen. I had a very important meeting with my director. . . .

"OKAY, NIKKI! WE'RE JUST GOING TO
FOLLOW YOU AROUND SCHOOL TODAY."

Well, EVERYONE in the ENTIRE school noticed my camera crew. And wherever I went, I was the center of attention.

The coolest thing was that everyone was SUPERnice to me, including the teachers. Probably because they wanted to make a really good impression on TV.

Of course, my BFFs and I were inseparable, as usual. I even asked them to be the costars of my show. We laughed, talked, and hung out like we always do.

For lunch, the director ordered burgers and cheese fries for us from Crazy Burger and sent her assistant to pick up the food!

And for dessert we had miniature gourmet cupcakes flown in from New York City from Baked by Melissa! OMG! They were SO yummy! I ate, like, sixteen of them.

But this is the crazy part! Kids were actually snapping pictures of me in the halls with their cell phones and asking me for my autograph during class.

I'm starting to feel like a REAL celebrity!

MacKenzie and the CCPs (Cute, Cool & Populars) are SO envious. They just stared at me and whispered. But I don't care! They're just mad because THEY'RE not the center of attention anymore.

I AM ☺!! Jealous much?!

My director said we'll be filming a total of eight episodes. And each one will be aired on TV a day or two after it's filmed. How COOL is THAT?!!

I'm totally LOVING this TV show stuff!

NOTE TO SELF:

Don't forget! Voice lesson TODAY with vocal coach from 5:00 p.m. to 6:00 p.m. I can hardly wait!

☺!!

NIKKI MAXWELL:
THE MAKING OF A POP PRINCESS!
EPISODE #1

POP PRINCESS
IN TRAINING!

TUESDAY, MARCH 11

My first voice lesson went really well yesterday! My teacher said I was a talented singer and a quick learner. SQUEEE!!! ☺!

Anyway, I was watching the movie *The Karate Kid* last night and thought, WOW! I wish I could do THAT!

By "THAT," I mean KARATE! Although the hero's first KISS was one of my favorite scenes too ☺! I'd LOVE being the fierce, fabulous, and feisty karate chick every girl wants to be and every guy wants to be with. MacKenzie would NEVER mess with me again. And Brandon would totally ask me to be his girlfriend! Hey, he'd be scared to death NOT to, because I could punch his lights out! Just kidding ☺!

Today the camera crew followed me to my gym class. Like the world needed to see me get slammed in the face (again!) playing dodgeball.

Anyway, as the old saying goes, "Be careful what you ask for, because you just might GET IT!"

Our teacher made a big announcement about our next activity. . . .

OKAY, CLASS, LISTEN UP. EXCITING NEWS! THIS MONTH WE'RE GOING TO BE LEARNING SELF-DEFENSE AND MARTIAL ARTS. PLEASE LINE UP TO PICK UP YOUR EQUIPMENT!

Then she gave everyone a karate uniform, called a gi. It came with a white belt since we were all beginners.

Chloe, Zoey, and I couldn't wait to put them on. Of course we looked AWESOME! Like real, live . . . girls in, um . . . karate uniforms.

Chloe came up with the crazy idea that we should work SUPERhard in class and earn our black belts by the end of the month. Then we can start a secret crime-fighting team called the Dorky Defenders! She said that superheroes lead very romantic lives, when villains aren't trying to KILL them. After hearing THAT little detail, I wasn't exactly sold on the superhero lifestyle.

Having to deal with MacKenzie is quite enough drama, thank you. I don't need any more villains sabotaging my life.

And speaking of sabotage, MacKenzie sashayed over and started HOGGING the camera. OMG! She looked like a HOT MESS!! . . .

She was dressed in a pastel pink gi that was trimmed
with ruffles and blinged out with rhinestones! She

had a matching monogrammed headband, pink platform shoes, and a shiny white leather belt.

It was quite obvious her nosy BFF, Jessica, who works in the office, had given her some inside information about our karate section in gym. And get this! She'd dusted her face and hands with pink shimmery glitter so she twinkled under the gym lights as she moved across the floor.

"K-I-A-I!" she screamed at the top of her lungs!

I was so startled by her sudden outburst that I peed my pants. Well, almost.

"What are you people staring at?" MacKenzie snarled. "Did you actually think I'd wear that hideous karate uniform? Not only is it three sizes too big, but the crotch of the pants hangs below your knees. Sorry! But you all are going to look like you've pooped your pants!"

"MacKenzie's such a spoiled DIVA!" Zoey whisper-giggled. "Someone needs to YIN her YANG!"

"Can you say SPARKLY. PINK. DISASTER?!!" Chloe laughed so hard she was snorting.

"Okay, class, that's enough! Please settle down!" our teacher scolded. "Our school has teamed up with a local karate school to add martial arts to our fitness program. So for the rest of the month, this class will be taught by an outside instructor who is an expert in the field. He'll be joining us tomorrow. I expect everyone to be courteous, respectful, and on their best behavior at all times. Understood?"

The entire class nodded. Except MacKenzie. She was sitting with her eyes closed, in a deep, tranquil meditation. Or taking a little nap. Personally, I think she was just showing off for the camera. That girl is such a DRAMA QUEEN!

Anyway, I think I'm really going to enjoy my martial arts class. My new black belt will look really cute with my black leather boots. I mean, how hard could it be?!

!!

102

We were just finishing our warm-up exercises in gym class when we heard a bizarre scream coming from the hall. "KIYAAAAAAAAAAA!!!!!"

Then this old guy with a potbelly charged through the doors! He was wearing a gaudy silver gi, and doing every corny Power Rangers fighting move he could think of!

He also has an overgrown, bushy mustache, but the biggest fail of all is his hair! It looks like he had it cut with a weed whacker while blindfolded.

WHAT was he thinking?! That hairstyle is so UGLY it has to be ILLEGAL in most states!!

After a minute of hollering, kicking, and flailing his arms like a crazy person, he was hoarse, out of breath, and completely worn out.

This dude took AWKWARD to a whole new level! Yet for some strange reason, I couldn't look away!

He coughed until he caught his breath. Then he dabbed his sweaty forehead with a silver hanky.

"Whew!" he panted. "Gimme . . . a second . . . !"

The entire class looked worried and alarmed. But it wasn't because our instructor appeared to be having a major heart attack right before our eyes. We knew it was going to be a LOOOONG month!

"Ha! I'm not winded! I was just . . . um . . . testing you! And you're just as GULLIBLE as I predicted!" he announced. "Let me introduce myself. I'm Rodney 'The Hawk' Hawkins, master of Hawk's High-Kick Karate School!"

He flexed his arms and showed off the hawk image on the back of his gi.

"As my students, you may address me as Sensei Hawkins, Fearless Leader, The King of Karate, or The Greatest Martial Artist OF ALL TIME!"

Ugh! His ego's almost bigger than that flabby gut hanging over his black belt, I thought.

"This isn't a gymnasium anymore, pip-squeaks, it's my karate dojo!" he shouted. "The Hawk doesn't tolerate weaklings in his dojo! I wanna see air punches right now! Watch me! One-two, one-two, one-two!"

He made us practice air punches until our arms almost fell off! . . .

ME, CHLOE, AND ZOEY
PRACTICING OUR AIR PUNCHES

However, my major concern was the TV crew televising a close-up of my sweaty armpit stains! EWW!

"It looks like some of you are slowing down," Sensei Hawkins yelled while sitting comfortably in a folding chair. "The Hawk doesn't tolerate laziness! Pick up the pace, or else!" He reached into his gi shirt and pulled out a bag of Cheeze E-O's cheese puffs.

"Is he seriously going to eat Cheeze E-O's during class?!" I asked Chloe and Zoey.

"I know!" Zoey agreed. "How he became a licensed fitness instructor is beyond me!"

"I dunno, maybe he's testing us again," Chloe said.

"The only thing the Hawk is TESTING is how good those Cheeze E-O's are!" I snarked.

He must have heard us or something, because he got up, walked over, and glared at us.

"HEY!" Chomp, chomp, chomp! "You three little pathetic princesses! More punching, less complaining!" he yelled, spitting cheesy orange specks everywhere. "The Hawk is NOT amused!"

US, COMPLETELY GROSSED OUT
BY OUR CRAZY TEACHER
SPITTING CHEEZE E-O'S ON US!

The only thing worse than spending an entire hour doing the same punch over and over is having to watch a sloppy karate instructor smack and snarf down more food!

After the Cheeze E-O's, he had beef jerky.

After the beef jerky, he had three candy bars.

After the candy bars, he had two bananas.

After the bananas, he had a bag of potato chips.

And after the potato chips, he had a dozen Oreo cookies.

And after the cookies, he had . . .

Wait for it . . . !!

Wait for it . . . !!

A DOUBLE CHEESEBURGER WITH BACON!!

"A burger?!" I uttered in disbelief. "This guy just pulled a BURGER out of his shirt! What is he hiding in there, a fridge or something?!"

"Who knows?" Zoey griped. "Let's just hope he doesn't have a jumbo-size combo meal in there! If he doesn't run out of food soon, he'll never dismiss this class! We could be stuck here the rest of the day."

"You're right, guys. This IS insane!" Chloe complained, rubbing her cramping arm. "Ouch! I am SO sore! And suddenly craving a burger!"

Luckily, Zoey (but unfortunately, not Chloe) got her wish! Sensei Hawkins savored the last crumb of his burger and wiped his dirty hands on his shirt.

"Hey! It looks like we're out of food . . . I mean . . . time!" he yelled. "I'll share a piece of karate wisdom with you before you go. A wise man once said, 'The only thing to fear is fear itself. But the only thing for fear itself to fear is . . . the Hawk!' HIYAAAAHHH!!!"

He tried to do a roundhouse kick, but HE couldn't get his leg very high because his overstuffed belly was in the way. So his kick was more of a punt.

By the end of class, Chloe, Zoey, and I were physically and mentally TRAUMATIZED.

Is THIS what karate is supposed to be like?!! Seriously! I'm SO over this martial arts stuff!

I have a better chance of defending myself with some of the ballet leaps I learned last fall. I'm just sayin' . . . !! ☹!!

But on a much happier note, I was practically mobbed at lunch today by the kids at school!

The first episode of my reality show, *Nikki Maxwell: The Making of a Pop Princess!* aired last night at 7:30 p.m., and everyone LOVED it.

OMG! I could barely eat my hot dog in peace.

Hey, I just might need to hire a security team like a real Hollywood TV star. They'd protect me from all of my ADORING fans at school so I can go to class every day. Poor ME!!

Anyway, my recording session was rescheduled just so my family and I could watch the show together. Mom even popped a big bucket of popcorn for us to share, like it was a blockbuster movie or something.

OMG! It was SO cool to see me and my BFFs on television. I have to admit, we were hilarious! I couldn't stop laughing! Chloe, Zoey, and I texted each other like crazy through the entire show.

My parents said they were really proud of me, and Brianna and Miss Penelope actually requested my autograph.

I can't wait to see the next episode! Although I'm totally bummed that I'll have to DVR it since I'll still be at the recording studio when the show comes on.

Thank goodness MY show doesn't have all the crazy drama, tears, screaming, backstabbing, and fighting, like all the others. I guess I'm just SUPERlucky!!

!!

NIKKI MAXWELL:
THE MAKING OF A POP PRINCESS!
EPISODE #2

KA-RAY-ZEE
KARATE CLASS

I've been DYING to know what Brandon wanted to ask me. Almost a week had gone by and he still hadn't mentioned it. Until TODAY!

In bio, he asked me to meet him at Fuzzy Friends after school tomorrow so we could talk. Even though I have a lot of stuff to do, I agreed. Then he smiled at me and blushed. And of course I smiled back at him and blushed. It was SO sweet!

Just like at the Sweetheart Dance! Um . . . did I ever mention that something happened that night at the dance?! No?

OMG! Everything was SO romantic. Just . . . PERFECT! It was just like a Disney movie. You know, when the handsome prince is about to kiss the beautiful princess. SQUEEEEEEE ☺!!

As we dreamily gazed into each other's eyes, a giant magnet seemed to be pulling us together! Closer, and closer, and closer. Until . . .

MacKenzie just came out of . . . nowhere!

Well, actually, that's NOT true.

Right before Brandon and I were so rudely interrupted, I smelled the foulest, FUNKIEST stench on the planet!!

And no! It was NOT Brandon's breath!

It was the aroma of 100% pure, grade-A Dumpster juice!

"STOP!! WHERE'S MY PRESENT?!" screeched a furious MacKenzie.

Her face was grimy, her hair was greasy, and her dress was covered in dark green slime!

"I've been digging around in that Dumpster for an hour. And my necklace is NOT in there! WHY did you LIE to me?!! Do I look STUPID to you?!"

"Well . . . ," I said, staring at the dirty toilet

paper hanging around her neck like a feather boa and the banana peel sliding down her forehead. "Um . . . are you SURE you want me to answer that question?"

"Shut up, Maxwell! LOOK what you did to me!" she screamed. "THIS is a designer gown identical to the one created for Taylor Swift. Now it's RUINED!"

I just rolled my eyes at that girl. Puh-lease! Can you say #RichGirlProblems?

That's when MacKenzie completely lost it!!

"I HATE you, Nikki Maxwell! I'm so angry . . . I could just . . . AAARRRGGGHHH!!!" she shrieked, and balled her fists.

Then she got all up in my face. "You might've won this battle, but the war is FAR from over!"

Then she attempted to sashay away on her broken platform heel, but it was more of a hobble, like *click, THUNK, click, THUNK, click, THUNK!*

Thank goodness she took that horrific smell with her.

OMG! Brandon and I were SO close to our first kiss!

If only MacKenzie hadn't barged in and interrupted us like that ☹!!

Unfortunately, the romantic mood quickly dissipated. But that Dumpster stench lingered on and on.

After the dance was over, Brandon walked me outside to the car. He told me he'd had a really great time. Then he said good-bye.

But one day our first kiss is REALLY going to happen. I just know it!

SQUEEE!!

☺!!

Today the camera crew filmed me practicing with my voice coach at the recording studio. At first I was really nervous about singing on camera. But after a while I hardly noticed them.

I'm already feeling tired, and next week is going to be even MORE hectic.

I have voice lessons daily, and filming three to four times a week. And the recording sessions start next Monday from 7:00 p.m. to 8:30 p.m., Monday through Friday.

And as if all of that isn't enough, Trevor Chase just asked Chloe, Zoey, and me to hold auditions for additional studio backup singers on Monday and Wednesday after school.

We also have a conference call with him next week to discuss adding a choreographer to our team, since we'll be opening for the Bad Boyz.

But the hardest thing so far has been trying to keep up with my classroom work AND get all of my homework done on time.

I've decided to go to bed an hour later at night and get up an hour earlier in the morning to make time to finish up my homework. Oh, crud! I just remembered I have a math quiz next week and I haven't even started studying for it yet.

I guess that means I should probably go to bed TWO hours later at night and get up TWO hours earlier in the morning.

To add to all of this craziness, I totally forgot I was supposed to meet Brandon after school today at Fuzzy Friends!

Lucky for me, the recording studio is only about four blocks from Fuzzy Friends. So I took off running like I was doing a marathon or something.

Just as I was approaching the building, Brandon was getting ready to lock up and leave. . . .

ME, RUSHING TO MEET BRANDON
AT FUZZY FRIENDS AFTER I'D
COMPLETELY FORGOTTEN ABOUT IT!

He looked really relieved and opened the door
for me.

"Sorry I'm l-late. Are you l-leaving already?" I panted,
completely out of breath.

"I was just about to. I've been here for two hours,"
he said, glancing at his watch.

OOPS ☹! I apologized profusely and explained
how, at the last minute, my voice instructor had
rescheduled to an earlier time so the camera crew
could film our session, and I didn't realize there was
a conflict until after the fact.

Brandon then explained that the thing he'd wanted
to talk to me about was a SUPERimportant project
he was working on. He needed me to help him with an
entry for a scholarship competition sponsored by the
Westchester Herald community newspaper. He says he
really needs the scholarship money to help pay the
tuition at our school. Boy, THAT problem sounds
vaguely familiar ☹!!

He has to submit six photos and an essay about an outstanding local student by Saturday, March 29. Which, BTW, is the same date as our listening party at Swanky Hill Ski Resort.

I was really flattered that Brandon chose ME for his entry!

So he'll be interviewing me about my life and future goals and taking photos of me working on my music and television projects.

Of course I said YES! Even though my schedule is already pretty crazy and will be getting worse.

We're going to meet in the library right after school on Monday.

To let him know just how committed I am to helping him on his project, I looked right into his beautiful brown eyes and PROMISED I'd be there for him. And that he could totally depend on me because I'd NEVER forget or be late AGAIN!

Hey! HE would have done the same thing for ME!

Anyway, in spite of the fact that I arrived late, Brandon and I had a blast hanging out with each other. He introduced me to two new playful puppies that had just arrived yesterday. . . .

A TERMINAL CASE OF PUPPY LOVE ☺?!!

But I had a really hard time trying to decide which was cuter and sweeter . . .

Those ADORABLE puppies . . .

Or BRANDON!!

SQUEEEEE!!

☺!!

NOTE TO SELF:

IMPORTANT! On, Monday, March 17, at 3:00 p.m. meet Brandon in the library to help him with his scholarship project! And PLEASE don't MESS this up!!

Today is my mom's birthday ☺! Happy birthday, Mommy!! I LOVE YOU!

I was surprised when my director called and requested permission to film at our home to capture this special Maxwell family moment. I wanted to say, "Sorry, but my family is NUTZ! VERY bad idea! NO WAY!"

But my mom was SUPERexcited about the idea. She went on and on about how she had always dreamed of having a healthy-food cooking show of her own for busy moms. And this was the closest she was EVER going to get to that dream.

I was like, JUST GREAT ☹!! But since Mom got all sappy and sentimental, I finally gave in and agreed. Of course, I have to admit, it really helped that:

1. Brianna was at a birthday slumber party and wouldn't be home until the afternoon. Which meant no embarrassing bratty little SISTER! Woo-hoo!

2. Dad was booked until noon with extermination appointments. Which meant no embarrassing DAD! Woo-hoo!

3. Our raggedy van was being driven by Dad. Which meant no embarrassing five-foot-long plastic ROACH! Woo-hoo!

Actually, this morning was the PERFECT time for the TV crew to come to my house and film since Brianna, Dad, and Max the Roach would NOT be home! My birthday present to Mom was breakfast in bed! So after I prepared her meal, I carried the tray up to her bedroom, shouted, "Surprise!" and sang "Happy Birthday."

"I love you, Mom!" I gushed. "Enjoy breakfast in bed with fresh strawberries on pancakes topped with extra whipped cream, and two scrambled eggs, bacon and sausage, milk, and orange juice! Just the way you like it!"

"Nikki, sweetheart! You shouldn't have!" she exclaimed, getting a little teary-eyed.

ME, SURPRISING MOM WITH BREAKFAST IN BED!

But OMG! She had NO idea how much trouble it was to make that breakfast.

It took me an hour just to learn how to flip pancakes. And another hour to scrape seven of them off the stove, floor, and ceiling. . . .

ME, TRYING UNSUCCESSFULLY
TO FLIP MOM'S BIRTHDAY PANCAKES!

After adding up the cost of the batter and other ingredients for all the wasted pancakes, and the two cans of paint to repaint the ceiling and walls, I could have cut my losses and just bought Mom an expensive designer scarf from an exclusive store at the mall.

Hey, you live and learn!

But most important, I helped my mom have a very happy birthday.

And the filming project with the TV crew went pretty smoothly too.

Woo-hoo!

NIKKI MAXWELL:
THE MAKING OF A POP PRINCESS!
EPISODE #3

TOTALLY
FLIPPING OUT

I spent most of the day trying to catch up on all of my homework. No matter how hard I try, I seem to be getting just further and further behind.

And right now I am SOOOO exhausted! I can BARELY keep my eyes open as I write this. . . .

ME, TRYING TO KEEP MY EYES OPEN EVEN THOUGH I'M EXHAUSTED!

I don't know how much longer I can keep up this crazy schedule.

And it's starting to STRESS me out ☹!!!!

I'm just SO tired! The ONLY thing I want to do is go to

137

Chloe, Zoey, and I were SUPERexcited about auditioning additional studio backup singers today after school and then going to the recording studio later.

We felt like we were famous celebrity talent show judges. You know, BEFORE they started scraping the bottom of the barrel and using those cray-cray celebs as judges.

But I guess Principal Winston didn't share our enthusiasm.

I asked him if we could hold our auditions in our brand-new state-of-the-art school auditorium. But he said it was only reserved for "special" events.

The worst place in our entire school is dingy sixth-grade classroom that smells like gerbil pee.

Well . . . unfortunately, THAT'S where he put us ☹!!

ME, TRYING REALLY HARD NOT TO SMELL
THOSE STINKY GERBILS

The kids auditioning either had superstrong willpower
or a very weak sense of smell.

Chloe, Zoey, and I actually learned how to be mouth
breathers!

"So, Tyrone, what brings you here today?" I asked the guy standing in front of us.

"I wanna be a backup singer. My voice is AWESOME, man!" he boasted. "I can outsing any of those famous boy-band dudes!"

"That's great! We can't wait to hear you," I said. "So, what are you going to sing for us?"

"You mean . . . like . . . right now?" He looked confused.

"Yeah. You do have a song prepared for the audition, right?" Zoey asked.

"No, man!" he answered. "I only sing in the shower. That's how I keep it real. Know what I'm saying?"

"No. Not really," Zoey said, rolling her eyes. "We're working in the studio right now, and this summer we may be doing some concerts. It would be kind of difficult for us to carry around a . . . um, SHOWER for you to sing in, Tyrone. . . ."

TYRONE, ONSTAGE WITH US WHILE
SINGING IN THE SHOWER!

"I only sing in the shower in MY bathroom, dawg, and that's it! All the stuff you're talking about is just . . . WEIRD!"

We watched in amazement as he headed for the door.

"Yo! If you can't get with the program, I'm outta here!"

"Well, that was productive!" I said with a frustrated sigh. "How many auditions have we seen so far?"

"Let's see! If we count all of the audition forms that you scribbled 'You gotta be kidding me ☹!!' on in red ink, crumpled, and then tossed in the wastebasket, I'd say we've had about twenty-nine auditions!"

Then Zoey looked at the callback tray.

"And judging from the number of callbacks, it looks to me like you absolutely, totally HATED all of the talent."

CALLBACKS

AUDITIONS

CALLBACKS

ZOEY, CALCULATING THE NUMBER
OF AUDITIONS AND CALLBACKS

"Ugh!" I slammed my head on the table. "This stinks!
Now I know why that Simon Cowell guy is so bitter all
the time!"

But as they say in Hollywood, THAT'S SHOWBIZ!

Well, some good news is that Chloe, Zoey, and I had our first recording session this evening at 7:00 p.m. It went really well. . . .

Not only do we sound great together, but we had a blast recording. And we did it all without having a shower stall in the studio. Sorry, Tyrone ☺!!

NIKKI MAXWELL:
THE MAKING OF A POP PRINCESS!
EPISODE #4

Well, my day got off to a pretty ROTTEN start ☹! When I woke up this morning, the most horrible thought hit me like a ton of bricks. . . .

OMG!! I TOTALLY forgot I was supposed to meet Brandon in the library after school yesterday!! I'm the worst friend EVER ☹!!

Even though I texted Brandon an apology, I was still an emotional WRECK! I felt so bad about the whole thing that I was distracted and spaced out the entire day.

And then in math class, I made a total FOOL out of myself during the quiz.

146

I really need to try to get more sleep! It's almost like I'm suffering from sleep deprivation or something.

I stayed up really LATE last night doing practice problems. Then I got up really EARLY this morning and did a few more.

The good NEWS is that all of that studying really paid off. I totally understood how to do those difficult equations and breezed right through the quiz.

However, the BAD news is that all of the stress about the Brandon situation combined with the lack of sleep finally took its toll on me.

I was so EXHAUSTED I could barely keep my eyes open.

The quiz question was:

Simplify the following algebraic expression:
$-2x + 5 + 10x - 9$

I just conked out right in the middle of the quiz!

And I must have drooled or something while I was snoozing because my answer was practically tattooed right across my face.

I had to go to the bathroom and wash it off with soap and water. But hey! At least it was the CORRECT answer!! Which means I got an A on the quiz!

Thank goodness the camera crew wasn't filming me today! I would have looked like a complete IDIOT!

OMG! When I saw Brandon in the hall before bio class today, I felt AWFUL! I apologized PROFUSELY for forgetting that we were supposed to meet in the library after school yesterday to work on his scholarship entry.

But get this! MacKenzie was hanging around SPYING on us. Like, WHO does that?!! She really needs to get a life and mind her OWN business! I don't know WHY she is so INSANELY jealous of my friendship with Brandon!

ME, APOLOGIZING TO BRANDON
(WHILE MACKENZIE EAVESDROPS
ON OUR CONVERSATION)

Anyway, I explained to Brandon that Trevor Chase had asked Chloe, Zoey, and me to conduct auditions for backup singers at the EXACT same time. And I didn't realize there was a scheduling conflict until AFTER the fact.

Brandon was supercool about the whole thing and said he'd already started working on writing the essay part about me.

He suggested that we reschedule for this Thursday, March 20. And of course I said YES!!

Anyway, I'm just happy Brandon isn't mad at me for standing him up like that.

He's, like, THE coolest guy EVER!

Unfortunately, the auditions we held today didn't go any better than the ones on Monday.

Even though we were looking for singers, we auditioned a comedian, a tuba player, two tap dancers, and a talking dog. Don't ASK!!

Suddenly my cell phone rang. I picked it up and cringed when I saw the caller's name.

"Oh no! It's Trevor Chase!" I groaned. "He probably wants to know how many new backup singers we've found from the people who came in for auditions!"

I took a deep breath and then clicked on the speakerphone.

"Hi, Mr. Chase! What a pleasant surprise to hear from you!" I said all perkylike.

"Do you have a second to talk?" he asked. "I won't keep you long. I know you're busy."

The room was as empty as a ghost town. I half expected to see a tumbleweed roll by! "Sure," I said. "I can spare a minute."

"Good. I have great news," Trevor said. "I've found the perfect dance choreographer! She's young, she's talented, she's hip, and she's assured me that she can have everyone whipped into shape and dancing like pros in no time at all!"

"That's awesome!" Chloe cheered.

"It sounds like she really knows her stuff!" Zoey gushed. "I'm totally on board with hiring her!"

"Me too," I agreed. "We're really excited to meet her!"

"Perfect! Because she's really excited about working with you," he said.

"OMG! What's that horrid smell?" MacKenzie shrieked as she entered the room. "They put you in the gerbil-pee room?! Disgusting!"

That's when she whipped out her expensive designer perfume. . . .

MACKENZIE, SPRAYING THE GERBIL
CAGE WITH DESIGNER PERFUME

Suddenly the stench in the room got even WORSE!

Thanks to MacKenzie, it now reeked of gerbil pee mixed with freshly picked roses. And just a hint of berries.

I shot her a dirty look.

"SHHHHH!!!!!" Chloe waved her hand at MacKenzie like she was shooing away an obnoxious fly.

"What are you doing here, MacKenzie?" I hissed, covering the phone with my hand.

"Checking out your little audition thingy," she answered. "That's strange . . . . I don't see anyone in line! Did I get here early, or is no one interested in joining your amateur, tone-deaf band?"

I honestly think MacKenzie has a homing device in her brain to find me when I'm miserable and make me feel ten times worse!

"If Trevor had chosen MY group for the record deal, the audition line would be a mile long!" She sneered.

"But he DIDN'T choose your band, did he?" Zoey shot back. "So cry yourself a river, build yourself a bridge, and get over it!"

"Actually, MacKenzie, we're really busy right now," I explained. "Mr. Chase has found us a choreographer who probably works with all of the biggest pop stars! Everything's going great for us, thank you. So please butt out of our business and go do something more constructive, like choke on a Tater Tot in the cafeteria!"

That's when MacKenzie's cell phone rang. Thank goodness! Now she could go blabber mindlessly to some other unlucky person. OMG! I had totally forgotten I still had Trevor Chase waiting on the phone.

"I'm so sorry about that interruption, sir!" I apologized. "Now, what were you saying?"

"We were talking about the choreographer. I'd like all of us to have a conference call," he said. "She has tons of ideas for you! Hang on, okay? I have her on hold!" After a couple of seconds I heard a few clicks.

"Hi, Mr. Chase!" the choreographer chirped.

"Hey! How's it going?" he replied. "Nikki Maxwell's on the line with us. Nikki, are you there? Can you hear us okay?"

"Yeah . . . but I'm picking up a weird echo," I answered.

"Really? How odd!" the choreographer said.

"There goes that echo again!" I frowned. "I don't know if my phone signal is bad or . . ."

That's when I noticed that Chloe and Zoey looked like they'd just seen a ghost or something! They nudged me and then nodded to my right.

"What's wrong, guys?" I asked, totally confused.

Then I finally SAW something VERY wrong . . . MACKENZIE ☹!!

She gave us a big phony smile, waved, and then said really sweetly . . .

YES, MR. CHASE! I'D LOVE TO WORK WITH THEM!!

US, IN SHOCK AT THE NEWS THAT MACKENZIE IS OUR NEW CHOREOGRAPHER

That's when I vomited a little in my mouth.

"So we're all in agreement, then. MacKenzie Hollister is your new choreographer," Trevor announced happily. "A teen choreographing a teen band!! I LOVE it!"

But I just kept my mouth shut so I wouldn't burst into an angry rant.

"Actually, Mr. C, we're classmates and locker neighbors!" MacKenzie giggled. "What a crazy coincidence! This is going to be SO much FUN!"

But Chloe, Zoey, and I could see her beady little eyes and that evil smirk on her face.

With MacKenzie on our team, this whole project is a train wreck just waiting to happen!

But the craziest part was THIS. . . .

MacKenzie announced that as our official choreographer hired by Trevor Chase, she would be giving us homework assignments that would make us stronger and better dancers.

MY first assignment was to watch a series of videos she'd made and posted on YouTube called The Fundamentals of Dance.

She said I was going to be practicing some of those same dance steps with her tomorrow after I finished working with my voice coach.

That's when I totally lost it and screamed, "MacKenzie, are you NUTS?! My schedule is already like a full-time job. If I get any busier, I'm going to have to drop out of middle school!!"

But I just said that inside my head so no one else heard it but me.

JUST GREAT! Now I can add watching MacKenzie's dance videos to my "Dumb Stuff I Gotta Do Tonight!" list.

Do all aspiring pop stars have to work with a calculating, maniacal . . . SOCIOPATH?!!!

!!

THURSDAY, MARCH 20

Today was a complete and utter DISASTER ☹!!

Thanks to MacKenzie, I was up until 2:00 a.m. last night watching her STUPID dance videos.

In one of them, she was dressed like a bumblebee and just danced around onstage for thirty minutes pretending to pollinate some fake plastic flowers.

Her dad must have hired someone to shoot those videos. Because no real audience would have sat there and watched that GARBAGE! I'm just sayin'!

And all day I was so tired I could barely keep my eyes open during class. This new schedule of mine is beyond exhausting.

Anyway, when the last bell rang, I rushed right over to the library to wait for Brandon. I actually got there a few minutes early. But I sort of accidentally fell asleep in a study cubicle. Well, that's what the librarian told me. . . .

162

BRANDON AND ME, PATIENTLY WAITING
FOR EACH OTHER IN THE LIBRARY
SO I CAN HELP HIM WITH HIS PROJECT

BRANDON, LEAVING THE LIBRARY AFTER
WAITING FOR ME FOR AN ENTIRE HOUR
(WHILE I SNOOZED IN A NEARBY CUBICLE)

That's what the librarian told me when she woke me up to tell me I had to go home because the library was closing in five minutes.

I can't believe I let Brandon down AGAIN ☹! His scholarship project is SUPERimportant!

If he UNFRIENDS me on Facebook, I'd TOTALLY deserve it!

Did I mention that I also slept right through my voice lesson? And my first dance practice with MacKenzie. It gets WORSE! My recording session starts in LESS than thirty minutes.

Which means I've been asleep in that stupid study cubicle for four hours!!

AAAAAAHHHHHHHHH!!!

(That was me screaming in frustration.)

NIKKI MAXWELL:
THE MAKING OF A POP PRINCESS!
EPISODE #5

I HATE, HATE, HATE my martial arts class ☹!!
I'm not very good at it. And my karate instructor
is CRAY-CRAY! He's always ranting about how he's
the "greatest" this and the "strongest" that. But
seriously, the only chops he knows about are PORK
chops!

In gym, Sensei Hawkins made us line up military style
with our hands at our sides. Then he paced the
floor, mean mugging random kids.

"So . . . . you little pip-squeaks have returned for
more of the Hawk's infinite knowledge," he said
mockingly. "Wise decision. It's a cruel, merciless world
out there! The 'eye of the tiger' philosophy will
only get you so far. But the 'claw of the Hawk'
conquers all! It's sharp, powerful, and hangnail free—
groomed with the nail clipper of RIGHTEOUSNESS!
AIIEEYAAA!!!"

He hollered, did a side kick, and tried to finish with
the splits. However, he only got about halfway down

before he stopped abruptly. Then he pursed his lips and tried NOT to scream in PAIN. . . .

THE HAWK DOES THE SPLITS?!

"Students . . . ," he announced, "what I'm REALLY demonstrating here is my signature Hawk's Wing Stance! I used this move to defeat a gang of eleven bank robbers, armed only with my bus pass, a bottle of prune juice, and an empty Doritos bag!"

Chloe, Zoey, and I exchanged looks and then rolled our eyes in complete disgust.

"Perhaps one day, the Hawk will teach you this deadly stance. IF you prove yourselves worthy!"

When he jumped out of his "stance," his back went CRAACK!! He winced and did a cocky laugh.

"Now prepare yourselves, pip-squeaks! It's time to demonstrate what you've learned from the last class. Any volunteers?"

I tried to avoid eye contact. I was praying that if I was still enough, I'd blend in with the deflated basketball behind me. I heard Sensei Hawkins sniff the air and walk toward me.

"The Hawk's keen nose is picking up the scent of a COWARD! Right . . . about . . . HERE!" he snarled, and pointed at ME!

"All right, puny coward, throw a good punch or you dishonor this dojo!!" he screamed right in my face.

THE HAWK, YELLING AT
ME TO PUNCH!!

That guy really needed to back off! I'm seriously allergic to big ugly JERKS.

The odor he was smelling was probably the liverwurst and tuna fish sandwich I smelled on HIS breath.

Then he pulled a pink cupcake out of his shirt, stuffed it into his mouth, and chomped angrily at me. The merciless chewing and smacking had me sweating bullets!

Then came the meanest, most threatening belch I'd ever heard! Even though it smelled like strawberries, he REALLY meant business!!

"Start punching!" he ordered.

I was so nervous, I actually forgot HOW to punch. I just stared at him blankly and tried really hard not to lose my breakfast.

"Did the Hawk give you permission to EYEBALL him?! NO! Just PUNCH!" he roared.

His face was really red. It made me think he was going to turn into the Hulk or something! But I guess his anger just made him want to eat more.

Before I could say "all-you-can-eat," he was holding a chocolate shake with whipped cream and a cherry on top. How is he storing that stuff?!

He must be some kind of magical FOOD WIZARD!

I FINALLY remembered how to punch and made a feeble attempt at an uppercut.

"NO!" He scowled with chocolate dripping from the corners of his mouth. "You call that powerful?! Roar when you punch, pip-squeak! Like this—HIIIYAAAAAH!"

"Oh, okay! Um . . . hi-ya!" I threw a weak jab and smiled nervously.

"NO! NO! NO!" he screamed, and stomped. "WHAT'S WRONG WITH YOU?! DO IT AGAIN!"

The other kids looked almost as scared as I was.

Chloe covered her eyes. "This is too much for me! I can't watch!" she whimpered.

Zoey bit her nails. "Be strong! You can do it!" she mouthed to me.

MacKenzie had this smirk on her face and was enjoying every minute of my public humiliation.

I closed my eyes, balled up my fist, and gave myself a pep talk. "Get it together, Maxwell! Throw a good punch or this guy is going to FAIL you! Think claw of the Hawk . . . claw of the Hawk . . ."

"Oh, look! The puny coward is tired!" he heckled me. "Anyone who takes a nappy-wappy in front of the Hawk gets nightmares! You hear that, pip—"

"HIIIIIYAAAAAAAH!" I screamed, and swung my fist as hard as I could.

CRUNCH!!!!!!!!

There was a collective gasp from the class. That's when I opened my eyes to see what had happened. Sensei Hawkins was lying on the floor, covered in his chocolate shake!!

"OOOOOWWW!" he moaned, rubbing his cheek.

"OMG! SENSEI!" I cried. "I am SO sorry! My eyes were closed when I punched! I didn't see you!"

I felt terrible! Sure, I wanted him to shut up. But not like that! I tried to help him, but he insisted on getting up by himself.

"No . . . big deal," he said in a weak voice. "That didn't hurt at all! Ha-ha! OWW!" He grabbed his jaw.

Poor guy! I think I accidentally bruised his face. And his ego! The saddest part was that I made him spill that yummy chocolate shake he was slurping down. I felt morally obligated to buy him another one.

Although, I had to admit—it WAS a pretty good punch! Strong and powerful! Just like the Hawk!

NOT!! I just hope he gives this "puny little pip-squeak" a passing grade.

!!

"Good morning, dear!" Mom chirped as I dragged myself into the kitchen.

It was 7:00 a.m. and she had on a fancy ruffled apron with cupcakes on it and a matching chef hat. Plus, she was wearing jewelry and makeup. It was definitely a huge change from her normal sleepy, disheveled look and ratty bathrobe.

"Good morning," I muttered, glancing at the clock. The film crew was supposed to arrive in an hour.

"Since you'll be filming today, I thought I'd make up a batch of my secret recipe—yummy organic cupcakes!" she said, picking up a silver tray filled with cupcakes and flashing me a huge megawatt smile. "They're the perfect high-energy snack for SUPERbusy moms and kids and ONLY three hundred calories! Preparation time is twenty-eight minutes."

"Mom, are you feeling okay?" I said, narrowing my eyes at her. She was acting a little strange.

"MY favorite is the delicious garbanzo bean with organic gooseberry icing," she said in a perky TV-chef voice. "The taste will knock you right off your feet! Why don't you try one, Nikki?"

ME, A LITTLE AFRAID TO TRY ONE OF MOM'S WEIRD, NASTY-LOOKING ORGANIC CUPCAKES

I just stared at it suspiciously. Garbanzo beans? And what exactly is a gooseberry? Finally I shrugged.

"Um . . . OKAY," I answered, and took a huge bite.

UGH! ICK! It was NASTY!

It would knock you off your feet, all right. Right onto the floor, writhing in pain with horrible stomach cramps from the yuckylicious taste!

"So, what do you think?" Mom asked anxiously.

I forced my trembling lips into a fake smile and just gave her a thumbs-up instead of the truth.

Why? I was afraid to actually open my mouth due to the high risk of involuntary projectile vomiting.

Sorry, Mom ☹!!

"I knew you would love it!" Mom gushed happily. "Just wait until you try my tuna-eggplant cupcake with oatmeal mustard frosting!"

Just the mention of those foul ingredients made me gag. AGAIN!

"No more, Mom! PLEASE!" I muttered as my stomach churned like a garbage disposal.

Before she could hand me the lump of purple goo covered in slimy oatmeal, my dad suddenly came running into the kitchen like his hair was on fire or something.

He was wearing a tacky-looking brown costume with a long cape and mask. And he had huge plastic bug antennae sticking out of his cap!

OMG! My dad looked like a cross between a slightly deranged superhero and a giant half-human cockroach!

For a moment I thought he was Max the Roach's long-lost father!!

Then Dad sprayed me with his bug sprayer thingy and hollered . . .

"Hey, it's ME! Like my new costume?" he chuckled.

"OMG! Dad, what's that HORRID smell?! A dead walrus?!" I shrieked.

And what lamebrained, immature IDIOT would be recklessly spraying it on people? I'm just sayin'.

"I should ask you, Nikki," Dad said. "I found a bottle of it under the kitchen sink. YOU said it was a homemade insect repellent/vinaigrette salad dressing/air freshener called Sardine Summer Splash! Remember your extra-credit gym project?"

Okay! So it was MY leftover fairy repellent spray that I'd made back in October! NEVER MIND!!

"This stuff works great!" Dad said. "It's totally safe. Kills bugs dead. And tastes good too!" He squirted some into his mouth. "So, when is the TV crew supposed to be here?"

Finally I couldn't take it any longer. "Mom! Dad! Why are you guys dressed up like this and acting like characters from some weird 1980s TV show?!" I yelled at them.

"Honey, haven't you heard the great news? Your show is doing so well that your producer wants to audition US for our own SPIN-OFF shows!" Mom said excitedly.

MY SHOW WILL BE CALLED THE EXERMINATOR!

AND MY SHOW WILL BE CALLED CRAZY CUPCAKE CREATIONS!

JUST GREAT!! My life is already a HORROR show. And now my parents are joining the cast?!

What's NEXT . . . ?!!

That's when Brianna and Miss Penelope came dancing into the room.

Brianna was wearing a tutu, a feather boa, Mom's heels, jewelry, sunglasses, and way too much makeup.

OMG! She looked like a five-year-old Katy Perry!

She was blasting an obnoxious song from Princess Sugar Plum's greatest hits collection and singing along, very off-key. . . .

"ROW, ROW, ROW YOUR BOAT, BABY! GOTTA ROW TO THAT FUNKY BEAT, BABY!" she howled. "DANCING DOWN THE STREEEEEEEAM!"

"Brianna! WHAT are you doing? And WHY are you dressed for a clown beauty pageant?" I asked, covering my ears so they wouldn't bleed.

"Wait a minute! You CAN'T call your show _Brianna's Got Talent!_" I protested. "What if someone comes along more talented than you and wins?"

"Me and Miss Penelope are the judges. And we'll always pick ME to be the WINNER! That's why it's called _BRIANNA'S Got Talent!!_ Not OTHER PEOPLE _Got Talent!_" Brianna said smugly, and then very rudely stuck her tongue out at me.

When she started singing again, I covered my ears. But I wanted to cover my eyes when she actually started doing the CHICKEN DANCE! I couldn't believe it when Mom and Dad started dancing and singing along.

"OMG! STOP IT! PLEASE!!" I screamed over the racket. "You're ALL driving me KA-RAY-ZEE!"

I snatched Brianna's music player and shut it off.

"When the TV crew gets here, they're going to think they walked into an insane asylum!" I yelled. "What is WRONG with you people?!"

That's when Mom, Dad, Brianna, and Miss Penelope glared at me in silence like I had totally lost it. . . .

MY ENTIRE FAMILY, EYEBALLING
ME ALL EVIL-LIKE!!

Okay! So maybe I WAS overreacting a little bit.

"Nikki, I'm really worried about you," Mom fretted.
"I think your hectic schedule is really stressing you
out. You've not been yourself lately. Would you
like this liver-'n'-onions cupcake with pickle relish
frosting? It'll help you relax, dear."

That's when I threw up in my mouth a little.

"Someone needs her beauty sleep!" Dad teased. "Just
go back to bed and sleep it off, sport! We'll let you
know when the TV crew gets here."

"Yeah! You're no fun at all when you're GRUMPY!"
Brianna said, and stuck her tongue out at me.
Again.

JUST GREAT! All of a sudden, everything
was MY fault! Like I was the CRAZY one! I
stormed upstairs to my room and slammed my door.
I'd had enough of that stupid reality show invading
my privacy and ruining my life! I stared at my piggy
bank. I could bust it open and scrounge up enough

loose change for a mustache disguise and a one-way bus ticket to somewhere far, far away. Like . . . um, SIBERIA!

That's when the craziest idea popped into my head. And no! My crazy idea WASN'T trying to take a BUS across the ocean to Siberia wearing a mustache disguise.

It was a DIABOLICAL plan that would:

1. SCARE that TV crew so badly that they'd NEVER, EVER want to set foot in this house again

AND

2. KILL all of those silly ideas about spin-off TV shows.

I'm such an EVIL GENIUS that sometimes I scare MYSELF!! MWA-HA-HA-HAA!

Gotta go now! I'll finish writing about this later. . . .

☺!!

OMG! You will never believe what happened here yesterday! It was UNREAL!!

I had less than fifteen minutes to come up with a plan to get rid of the TV crew. I crept downstairs and snuck up on Brianna, who was watching cartoons in the living room.

"Pssst!" I whispered. "Pssst! Brianna!"

"Miss Penelope, would you PLEASE stop bugging me!" she said, rolling her eyes at her hand. "You can watch the news after this cartoon is over!"

"No! It's ME!" I snapped. "Look behind you, dummy! I mean . . . dear!"

"Oh! Hi, Nikki! Why are you whispering?" Brianna asked. "Are you playing a game? CAN I PLAY?!"

"Shhhhh!" I covered her mouth. "Yes! But you have to be superquiet. It's a secret game, okay?"

She nodded.

"Let's sneak upstairs and I'll explain," I whispered. "I don't want Mom and Dad to hear. Okay?"

She nodded again, and I slowly removed my hand from her mouth.

"NIKKI, I CAN'T WAIT TO SNEAK UPSTAIRS TO PLAY OUR SECRET GAME!" she screamed excitedly. "I PROMISE I WON'T TELL MOM AND DAD A THING! AND, MUH, MUH, MUH, MUH . . ."

I didn't have a choice but to slap my hand back over her mouth to shut her up. The last thing I needed was for Brianna to ruin my plan by blabbing everything to Mom and Dad. With my hand still over her mouth, I picked her up like a human football and ran up the stairs like I was trying to score a touchdown or something! After we'd made it safely to my room, I sat her on my bed and scolded her.

"Brianna! The first rule about the secret game is, WE DON'T TALK ABOUT THE SECRET GAME!"

"My bad!" she giggled. "Sugar makes me chatty."

"Anyway, I have fab news! I've got a plan for how YOU and Miss Penelope can get your own TV show!"

"REALLY?!!!" she shouted. "I'M SOOO HAPPY!"

I shushed her and continued. "Talent shows are so . . . yesterday. You need to impress the director with something she's never seen before."

"Okay!" Brianna said excitedly. "So, um . . . what exactly has she never seen before?"

"Well, you could wear your cute red heart pj's! And paint cute red polka dots on your face. We'll call your style . . . um . . . cute clown couture!"

"What?! Pj's and polka dots?!" she said, scrunching up her nose. "Hmm! I think that's . . . AWESOME! I love clowns! Well, except for the creepy, sad ones. Those guys are scary! I'm not going to be a creepy, sad, scary clown, am I, Nikki?!"

"Of course not!" I assured her. "I have a strict no-creepy-sad-scary-clowns-allowed policy."

Brianna changed into her pj's and I got busy with the polka dots. . . .

ME, HELPING BRIANNA GET HER
VERY OWN TV SHOW (KIND OF)

"There! All done! See how cute you look?!"

"Hey! Wait a second!" Brianna said, examining her face in the mirror and frowning. "Are you kidding me? How am I supposed to get a TV show looking like this?!"

Oh, crud! She wasn't drinking the Kool-Aid! Brianna pointed at her cheek. "Nikki, you missed a spot! Right there! See?"

"Oh. Sorry about that!" I replied sarcastically. I added one last red polka dot to her cheek.

"There! Now it's perfect!" She smiled. "I'm going to be a famous reality TV star. Just like Honey Boo Boo!"

I breathed a sigh of relief.

"Oh! I almost forgot! I need a funny name, too," Brianna said.

I had the PERFECT name for her!

I whispered it into her ear and she couldn't stop giggling.

Suddenly the doorbell rang. Yikes! The TV crew had finally arrived.

I said a prayer that my plan would work.

"Okay, let's go! And remember, Brianna, you're a STAR! Now sparkle . . . !"

I rushed downstairs and opened the door.

"Good morning, everyone! Come right in!" I said, and plastered a fake smile on my face.

That's when my director noticed Brianna. "Hello, sweetheart! What's your name?"

"It's CHICKEN POX!" Brianna yelled. "Isn't CHICKEN POX a silly name?! I got these cute red polka dots this morning. Aren't they booty-ful?"

That's when the entire TV crew gasped. . . .

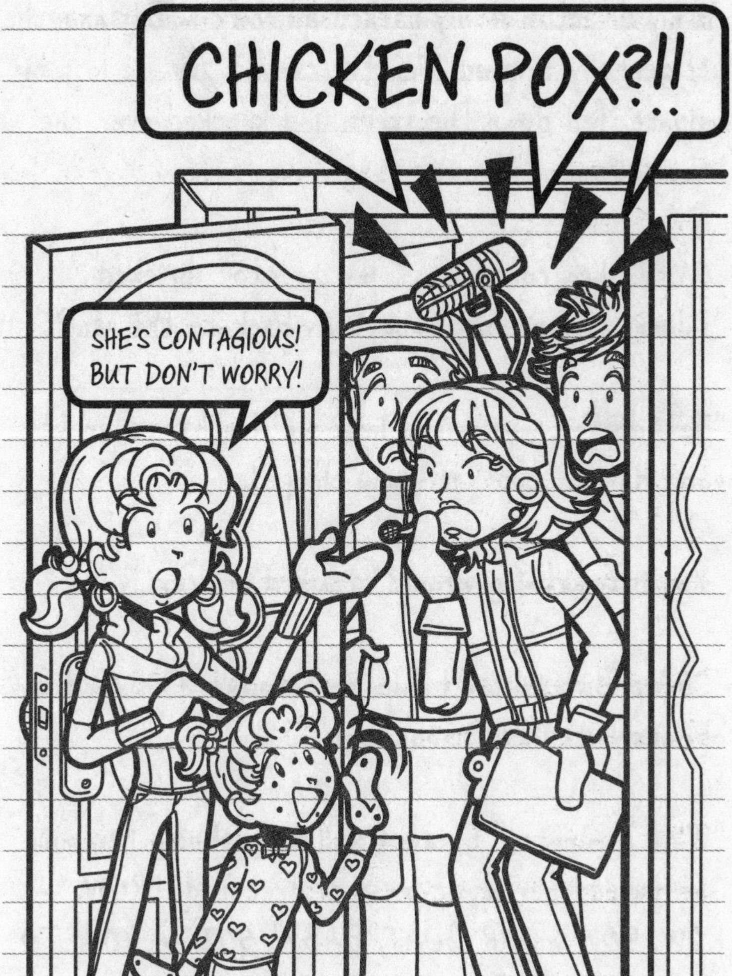
CHICKEN POX?!!
SHE'S CONTAGIOUS! BUT DON'T WORRY!

As my director slowly backed away from Brianna, she accidentally tripped over the camera guy. He lost his balance, fell down the steps, and knocked over the lights guy.

"OMG! She's contagious!" my director shrieked. "Filming is canceled! Everybody back to the van!"

"Hey, do you guys wanna hear me sing?! I'm a pretty good dancer, too!" Brianna chirped.

"Um, is something wrong?" I asked innocently.

"Sorry! But we can't film here today. This child is obviously very sick! Good-bye!"

"Wait a minute!" Brianna yelled, grabbing her mic. She turned her music on and screeched, "ROW, ROW, ROW YOUR BOAT, BABY! GOTTA ROW TO THAT FUNKY BEAT, BABY!"

The entire TV crew took off running down the sidewalk, back to their van, dropping equipment along the way. Brianna ran after them, singing,

"DANCING DOWN THE STREEEEEEEAM!"

OMG! It was a scene straight out of a comedy movie. If only I'd had a camera to film it all.

If I hadn't intervened, I'm sure each of my family members would have gotten their own TV show, including Miss Penelope.

My life has been a wreck these past few weeks due to my superbusy schedule. And I'm not about to stand by and let this happen to my family. Sure, they're a little cray-cray! But they're mine! And I LOVE them!

I'm really sorry to disappoint my director and all of those TV viewers. BUT . . .

What HAPPENS in the Maxwell residence STAYS in the Maxwell residence!!! ☺!!

Anyway, thank goodness my fake Chicken Pox Apocalypse worked like a charm! That TV crew won't be coming back to my house anytime soon.

NIKKI MAXWELL:
THE MAKING OF A POP PRINCESS!
EPISODE #6

CANCELED
THE CHICKEN POX
APOCALYPSE

I feel really bad about not being more supportive of Brandon and his scholarship project.

I know what it feels like to be SUPERworried about how your tuition is going to get paid. Been there, done that! Got the T-shirt!!

I just hope he's not at risk for having to transfer schools ☹!! I need to talk to Brandon today to find out when we can meet again so I can help him.

Anyway, I was a little nervous about showing my face in my martial arts class today. Hey! You'd feel a little AWKWARD too if you'd almost knocked out your teacher!

And it didn't help matters when I saw MacKenzie and Jessica whispering about me and giggling.

OMG! I CRINGED when I actually saw Sensei Hawkins. It looked like someone had toilet-papered his face or something!

Come on! The punch wasn't *that* hard. Were the ten rolls of bandages really necessary?! Or the three pints of assorted Ben & Jerry's ice cream flavors he'd piled on a waffle cone?!

"Listen up, pip-squeaks! Being a karate master isn't just about kicks and . . . um, PUNCHES," the Hawk said, glaring at me. "It's about a killer instinct!"

In spite of his tough talk, I could have sworn he flinched when I suddenly leaned forward and sneezed. He almost dropped his ice-cream cone.

"You have to be wise and clever to outsmart your enemy. For instance, take these bandages!" He pointed at his head. "They're FAKE! I'm just using them to make a point. Got it? In real life, you'll never see bruises on the Hawk, because they're too SCARED to show up!"

He did a three-punch combo and yelled, "HIIIIIIIII-OOOUUCH!!" Then he grabbed his jaw and whimpered in pain like a small puppy. Next he made a very shocking announcement. . . .

ME, IN SHOCK OVER THE FACT THAT
WE'RE HAVING A POP QUIZ IN GYM!!

"And don't you DARE think it's because I'm sore or injured. Or that I'm PUNISHING the class for my, um . . . FAKE fractured jaw. I just wanna see if you have the knowledge required for a true martial arts warrior."

"What? No punching?" a boy in front of me grumbled sarcastically. "Why don't you spar with Knuckles Nikki today? That'll be fun!"

"Nah! He's probably afraid Muscles Maxwell will knock his lights out again!" the boy next to him snickered.

Knuckles Nikki?! Muscles Maxwell?!

I groaned and buried my face in my hands.

Hey, call me a DORK! But NEVER, EVER call me those names! It makes me sound like a heartless THUG or BULLY!!

"It's okay, Nikki," Chloe said, patting my shoulder sympathetically. "Look on the bright side. With your new rep, you won't be the first person eliminated in dodgeball anymore! Everyone will be scared to death to hit you!"

"Hmm. Actually, that would be nice . . . ," I mused.

Wait a minute, WHAT was I saying?!!!

"I'm NOT that type of person!" I muttered. "It was all an accident, people! An ACCIDENT!!"

"No talking, pip-squeaks! The Hawk better not hear a pin drop!" Sensei said. "Now get to work so I can EAT this ice-cream cone before it melts! Er, I mean, um . . . MEDITATE . . . to become more awesomely powerful!"

When did a martial arts pop quiz become more difficult than a math one?! When I read over my quiz, I suddenly realized that everything I knew about karate I'd learned from the Disney and Nickelodeon channels and Saturday morning cartoons.

And unfortunately for me, it was all WRONG!! . . .

THE HAWK'S POP QUIZ   NAME: Nikki Maxwell

There are many different styles of martial arts.
Name at least 8:

OK
(Kung Fu) ~~Panda~~   OK ~~The~~ (Karate) ~~Kid~~ $\frac{4}{16}$ 🙁

X Ninjago   X Supah Ninjas

X The Last Airbender   X Power Rangers

X Mulan   X Teenage Mutant Ninja Turtles

What belt is the lowest rank, and what does it represent?

Seat belt – <u>lowers</u> the chance of injury in a car accident

Leather belt – can be worn <u>low</u> on your waist

Snowbelt – snow has a <u>low</u> temperature

Sunbelt – hot with a <u>low</u> chance of rain

Match the following words with their definitions:

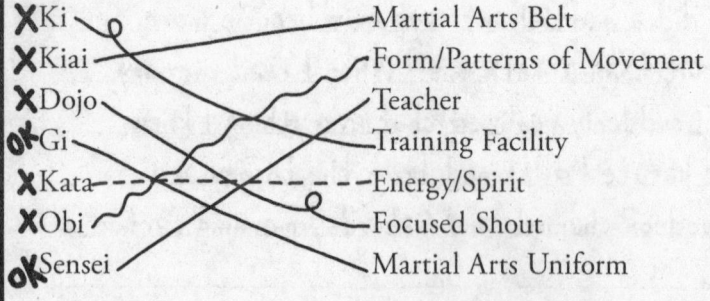

X Ki   Martial Arts Belt
X Kiai   Form/Patterns of Movement
X Dojo   Teacher
OK Gi   Training Facility
X Kata   Energy/Spirit
X Obi   Focused Shout
OK Sensei   Martial Arts Uniform

I guess I thought the questions were going to be SUPEReasy, like, "Who's your favorite Ninja Turtle?"

Wow! That quiz was really HARD!

If I want to pass this class and earn a belt, I'd better start studying for the final written test. It's on Friday, which means I only have ~~five~~ four days left to prepare for it!

I guess I'll be adding THIS to the long list of Stuff That I'm Way Too Busy to Get Done So Why Even Bother to Try!!

☹!!

AAAAAAAHHH!

(That was me SCREAMING ☹!!)

OMG! Am I becoming a TOXIC friend?!! Like in those over-the-top teen TV dramas with the sappy emo music? You know, where the dimwitted teen drama queen accidentally-on-purpose ruins her chances with the guy of her dreams.

Only to HATE herself for it later!!!

Then she whines obnoxiously all day long about the relationship that SHE torpedoed. And feels so pathetically sorry for herself that you just want to PUKE!

Or change the channel. Or BOTH!!

I'm really worried about my friendship with Brandon.

I need to talk to him and apologize again for being too busy to help him with his scholarship project.

Oh! And for standing him up last week.

And for um . . . falling asleep in the library. While he waited for me, like, FOREVER!!

ARGH ☹!!! I'm such a HORRIBLE friend. And Brandon deserves better.

Lately, I've just been reliably UNRELIABLE. And the guilt is totally eating me up inside ☹.

I really think I should talk to my BFFs, Chloe and Zoey. I'm sure they can help me with my Brandon problem. They always do!

Anyway, I was waiting for my BFFs when suddenly MacKenzie walked up to me and got all up in my face.

Then she actually started screaming at me. . . .

I was already in a pretty cruddy mood. So I looked right into MacKenzie's beady eyes and told her off really good!

"Okay, MacKenzie! Here's my excuse. . . . My CRAZY choreographer had plenty of time to tell me about a MORNING practice when she forced me to rehearse until ten o'clock last NIGHT! But instead, she decided to call me at six o'clock this morning, while I was in the shower, and leave a message that I just got ten minutes ago! Which was fifteen minutes AFTER the practice was OVER!"

"Well, you'd better make up that practice or I'll call Trevor Chase!" MacKenzie threatened.

"Actually, MacKenzie, go right ahead! You can call the TOOTH FAIRY for all I care! I barely have time to breathe. So I can't just drop everything anytime YOU get the whim to torture me with an unscheduled dance practice. Sorry, but I'm NOT giving YOU the pleasure of giving ME a nervous breakdown! I know you're trying to make me quit so you can take over my band AND my TV show!"

"So, are you done with your delusional little rant?! It's not totally MY fault that your life's a wreck!" MacKenzie sneered and narrowed her icy-cold blue eyes at me. Then she just stared at me for what seemed like FOREVER! I could tell the gears were turning in that tiny brain of hers. She was up to something!

"Actually, Nikki, you're right! You DO need a break. I've been pushing you too hard. So dance practice is canceled for the rest of the week!"

"WH—WHAT?!" I sputtered. My mouth dangled open in complete shock.

"I said, I'm giving you the week off! You know the choreography so well you could do it in your sleep. And believe me, I've actually seen you do it in your sleep! Use the time off to get some rest!"

Before I could say a word, MacKenzie turned and sashayed down the hall. I just hate it when that girl sashays! No dance practice?! That was too good to be true! I could apologize to Brandon at lunch today and offer to help him with his project. I was starting to think maybe MacKenzie wasn't such a WITCH after all. That is, UNTIL she HIJACKED my TV crew!!

A large crowd of kids gathered to watch as she continued. "I can't say much because this is a personal matter. But I feel SO sorry for her. Especially since she's in this messy LOVE triangle with a member of her band. He's secretly crushing on another girl who's WAY out of Nikki's league. And Nikki's insanely jealous. Sorry, that's all I can reveal at this time."

The director's eyes lit up. "Now, THIS is the stuff we've been waiting for. Conflict between band members! Turmoil! Heartbreak! Intrigue! Get a close-up of her, Steve! And and keep the camera rolling."

The camera guy quickly zoomed in on MacKenzie's face for dramatic effect. She batted her eyes all innocentlike and then took out her Raging Revenge Red lip gloss and applied, like, seven layers.

"Go ahead and vent, sweetie! You'll feel so much better! You obviously really care about your friend Nikki," the director said, egging her on. "Now, what can you tell us about this other band member?"

MacKenzie sighed deeply and then dabbed at phony tears to heighten the drama.

"Well, I'm not one to spread gossip, but he and Nikki are in this on-again, off-again relationship. OMG, it's SO dysfunctional! All they do is argue, and Nikki is fed up. I have a really bad feeling she's going to dump him tomorrow. Or he'll dump HER as soon as he sees all of this dirt aired on TV! It's going to be AWFUL! Awfully JUICY!"

I could NOT believe that girl was LYING on camera like that! Has she no SHAME?!! OMG!! I had to restrain myself from walking over and wiping that little smirk off of her!

MacKenzie stared into the camera, pretending to be distraught. "I'm warning you! Soon you're going to be up to your eyeballs in drama. I'm concerned it could damage Nikki's music career and be extremely mortifying for BRANDON."

Then she placed her hand over her mouth in mock dismay. "OOPS! Did I just reveal his NAME?! I've already said way too much! And as a friend, I feel it's important to respect their privacy. Sorry!"

"Actually, your observations have been very insightful!" the director gushed. "The ratings for this episode are going to be through the roof! It just might win me an Emmy Award!"

MacKenzie smiled, batted her eyelashes, and twirled her hair around and around and around. She was obviously trying to hypnotize the director into doing her evil bidding. I KNEW what she wanted.

"Well, I think you deserve an award! So how about a TV show about ME and my VERY fabulous life? I'm a SUPERtalented dancer and fashion designer, and my aunt Clarissa owns the—"

But the director totally ignored her blabbery. "Okay, guys, listen up! Tomorrow we keep a camera on Nikki every minute of the day. Don't let her out of your sight, understand? And we'll need a second camera to follow that Brandon kid around. Somebody get me a copy of his class schedule!"

Suddenly I felt SICK to my stomach.

Right now I'm hiding out in the library, writing all of this in my diary. Thank goodness I'll be leaving school for a dentist appointment in fifteen minutes. I'm still in shock that MacKenzie would actually do something so VILE!

I have no choice but to try to warn Brandon! Before it's too late!! ☹!!

I don't know if I'll EVER recover from MacKenzie's outrageous little stunt. For her to portray Brandon as some heartless dude in a crazy, drama-filled love-triangle with me and MacKenzie was just AWFUL!

My plan was to avoid the TV crew the entire day, then ditch them and secretly meet up with Brandon after school. However, I STILL needed to WARN him! Although, with all of the gossip going around, there was a good chance he'd already heard that the TV crew was planning to hunt him down like an animal. Poor guy ☹!

Before going to class, I decided to stop by my locker and grab ALL my books. I knew the FIRST place they were going to look for me was at my locker, so it was the LAST place I wanted to be.

I hid out in the janitor's closet until the halls were completely empty. Then I practically tiptoed to my locker. My plan was going really well until . . .

Oh, CRUD!! Suddenly I was surrounded! I'd been CAPTURED! Like a frightened little MOUSE in the deadly grip of a steel TRAP! However, unlike the mouse, I unfortunately didn't have the option of chewing off my own leg to escape ☹! Sorry, but I was desperate.

"Hi, Nikki! You're on camera!" my director said. "Today we're using cue cards to help you tell your story. Just read them and make us feel your pain. Okay?"

"We're using cue cards?" I glanced at the one an assistant was holding up and read it out loud. "It's finally over between Brandon and me . . . ?! What?!"

Okay, this was getting out of control. "Actually, that's not true. Um, can we turn off the camera for a minute? There's no way I can say that!"

"Well, you just did! And with a little editing, it'll be perfect. Keep up the good work!" my director said happily.

OMG! I was SO ticked off! It was quite obvious that calm reasoning was not going to get me very far with these people. I decided it would be smarter to just pretend to cooperate. It had worked like a charm on Saturday. My biggest regret was that I HADN'T brought my red paint to school with me today. Then I could have TERRORIZED the TV crew with the Chicken Pox Apocalypse, Part 2 ☺!

"So, when are you going to dump that guy Brandon?" the director asked. "I was thinking we could do a wide-angle shot and add some emo music to help set the mood. This breakup is going to be AMAZING! No offense. . . ."

"Um, actually, I have class right now! But we can meet right here at my locker afterward," I lied.

"Sounds good! We'll be waiting," the director said, and gave me a thumbs-up.

My mind was racing as I trudged off to class. It was almost impossible to concentrate on the lesson, and each minute seemed like an hour. But as soon as the bell rang, I rushed into the hall in search of Brandon. I had to warn him. I just hoped it wasn't too late.

I collapsed against a wall, out of breath, and checked for signs of the TV crew. They were probably STILL waiting for me at my locker.

I peeked around the corner and spotted Brandon just as he was leaving his locker. I couldn't help but notice that he looked kind of down. . . .

I felt another pang of guilt for being such a cruddy, inconsiderate friend.

"Brandon!" I yelled, and waved to get his attention. "Do you have a minute?"

He turned around, gave me a half smile, and shrugged. "Hi, Nikki. I have a math test next period. But I can spare a minute. What's up?"

"Actually, I owe you an apology for . . . um, everything! I know your project is SUPERimportant, and I want to help you try to win that scholarship money."

"Nikki, your schedule is wicked crazy. So I understand if you don't have the time to—"

"No, Brandon, there's no excuse for what I did. I'm truly sorry! And I really mean it. My dance practices have been canceled this week, so I have some extra time. I thought we could meet in the library to work on your project after school today and then hang out at Fuzzy Friends!"

He gave me a big smile and brushed his shaggy bangs out of his eyes. "That's cool! I really appreciate you wanting to help out with my project. I'm lucky to have a friend like you."

Try UNLUCKY! I looked over his shoulder and saw the camera crew marching down the hall. I didn't want them to see Brandon. And I definitely didn't want Brandon to see those crazy cue cards! I had to finish talking and get out of there. FAST!

"Thanks, Brandon, but please try to avoid the camera crew, because MacKenzie told them a bunch of lies and now they're looking for you good luck on your math test I'll talk to you later bye!"

Brandon looked totally confused. "What'd you just say? Wait! What about my project? And are we still meeting at Fuzzy Friends after—"

I left Brandon standing there. I blew past the camera crew, and they followed me just as I had planned. I cut through the cafeteria and ducked into the girls' bathroom near the gym. I dived into a stall and locked the door as my heart raced! But there was no getting away from that darn camera and the wacky cue cards. . . .

Everywhere I hid, the camera eventually found me.
Including the janitor's closet. . . .

Finally I gave up and just let the camera follow me around school. Which also meant I NOW had to stay clear of Brandon.

My situation was kind of depressing because, thanks to MacKenzie, I finally had some extra free time in my schedule.

But thanks to her little on-camera confessional, I couldn't EAT LUNCH with Brandon, TALK to Brandon between classes, WORK on Brandon's project in the library, or even HANG OUT with Brandon after school.

MacKenzie had managed to manipulate me AGAIN! And drive a wedge between Brandon and me.

Of course, I didn't help our situation any when I just disappeared into thin air and left him standing there in the hallway, flustered and confused.

After that little stunt, Brandon had every reason to avoid me like the plague. Hey! I was SO disgusted, I wanted to avoid ME too!

OMG! I was so upset, I wanted to cry. But I couldn't do THAT, either, with that stupid camera all up in my face!

I could hardly wait for the school day to FINALLY be over!

As soon as I got home, I ran up to my room, threw myself across my bed, and had a good cry. Then I just stared at the wall and sulked. Which for some reason always makes me feel a lot better.

Soon I fell asleep and had the most HORRIBLE nightmare! The scariest thing about it was that it felt SO real!

When I finally woke up, it was almost midnight. And since I was feeling better, I started writing in my diary. But then I had the weirdest feeling that something else was in the room with me.

Something VERY evil! And when I looked up, I actually saw it! _OMG!_ I was so TERRIFIED that I wanted to scream, but I COULDN'T. . . .

ME, HAVING A HORRIBLE NIGHTMARE
ABOUT THE TV CREW AND CUE CARDS!

Finally, I woke up for real and realized it was still all just a very bad dream. Thank goodness!

I was a little paranoid, though, so I checked under my bed and inside my closet for hidden cameras, crazy TV crews, and nasty cue cards. I'm thinking I'll probably just sleep with the lights on tonight. . . .

☹!!

NIKKI MAXWELL:
THE MAKING OF A POP PRINCESS!
EPISODE #7

CAN I HAVE A
LITTLE PRIVACY,
PLEASE...?!!

After I had that valentine confiscated in bio last month, you'd think I would have learned my lesson!

RIGHT? WRONG!!! I can't believe I came SO close to getting my CELL PHONE confiscated!

I was in math class, DYING to update Chloe and Zoey on the situation between Brandon and me.

And when my teacher instructed the class to take out our textbooks and our calculators, I knew it was the perfect opportunity to grab my cell phone and send them a text.

Hey, it DOES have a calculator! So why NOT? I figured as long as I raised my hand and gave her a few correct answers, my little secret would go unnoticed.

I was also being as careful as possible to follow the SGTCWGC, also known as the STANDARD GUIDELINES FOR TEXTING IN CLASS WITHOUT GETTING CAUGHT!

SGTCWGC GUIDELINES

HOW TO GET CAUGHT

1. Text and read texts openly in class.

2. Look at your phone and laugh.

3. Wear clothing without pockets.

4. Forget to silence your phone.

HOW NOT TO GET CAUGHT

1. Text without looking at your phone.

2. Sneak a peek at your phone and respond later.

3. Wear a sweatshirt with a front pocket or carry a purse to conceal your phone.

4. Know where your teacher is at all times.

It is VITAL that every kid who owns a cell phone AND texts during class knows these rules. Otherwise, you'll be at serious risk for a CPCBT, also known as CELL PHONE CONFISCATION BY TEACHER! Anyway, I decided to text Zoey and update her on Brandon and me. It went something like this:

* * * * *

Nikki: Hey! I need advice on what to do about Brandon.

Zoey: Spill!

Nikki: I think he's avoiding me! Probably because of the TV camera fiasco.

Zoey: R u kidding me?! But that was all MacKenzie's fault.

Nikki: Yeah, I know. I think I need to talk to him again.

Zoey: I agree! But what are you going to say?

Nikki: If $x = -4$, then $24 + 3 - 2x = ?$

Zoey: ?????

Nikki: Sorry! I'm in math class and using my phone as a calculator :-p!

* * * * *

"MISS MAXWELL! WHAT are you doing?!!"

My teacher was staring at me.

As I scanned the room I also noticed that the entire class was gawking at me too. It was HORRIBLE!

I knew I had to say something quick, so I just said the first thing that came to my mind.

"Um . . . using my calculator?"

"Then why is it vibrating?"

I racked my brain for a logical reason why a calculator would be vibrating.

"Um . . . how about it's really nervous because it doesn't know the answer to the problem?!"

My teacher frowned and started walking quickly toward me with her hand held out to do a surprise CPCBT (Cell Phone Confiscation By Teacher).

I panicked and froze like a deer in headlights.

That's when I remembered the most important SGTCWGC guideline of them all: What to Do in the Event of a Surprise CPCBT.

HANDLING A SURPRISE CPCBT

If a teacher ever approaches you and extends his/her hand for a CPCBT (Cell Phone Confiscation by Teacher), **_DO NOT GIVE UP YOUR PHONE!_** Instead, simply open your mouth, take out the gum you are chewing, and place it in the palm of his/her hand. S/he'll be SO utterly DISGUSTED s/he'll quickly FORGET the reason s/he approached you.

Unfortunately, I didn't have any gum.

I had given my last piece to Chloe after gym class earlier today ☹!

But lucky for me, I DID know where to FIND some gum in a middle school classroom ☺!

And LOTS of it.

As my teacher marched toward me, I quickly reached under my desk and grabbed the biggest wad of gum I could find.

And YES! It was REALLY, REALLY gross.

But . . .

I was REALLY, REALLY, REALLY
desperate NOT to LOSE my cell phone!

This is what happened. . . .

ME, GRABBING A HUGE, RANDOM,
REALLY GROSS WAD OF GUM
FROM UNDER MY DESK!

Then, with all eyes on me, I shoved that wad of gum into my mouth and started chewing away. . . .

ME, CHEWING A HUGE, RANDOM, REALLY GROSS WAD OF GUM FROM UNDER MY DESK!

My teacher gasped and stopped cold in her tracks! Then she looked like she was about to gag. Finally she regained her composure and just shook her head in disbelief. She walked to her desk, collapsed into her chair, and spent the rest of the hour trying in vain to figure out WHY she EVER chose to become a teacher.

I could hear the disgusted remarks of my classmates. But I didn't care.

I STILL had my phone ☺!!! WOO-HOO!

The MORAL of this story: If you text in class on a regular basis, ALWAYS follow the SGTCWGC. And most important, NEVER, EVER get caught without GUM! Because if you do, when your teacher comes to confiscate YOUR cell phone, you'll be forced to either:

1. CHEW a wad of gum from that HUGE, but very NASTY, emergency supply conveniently stuck under your DESK ☹!!

OR

2. LOSE your BELOVED cell phone ☹!!

Hey, the choice is YOURS!

Anyway, it's hard to believe our listening party is only two days away! I can hardly wait!

Even though I'm SUPERexcited about it, I still get this sick feeling in the pit of my stomach whenever I think about the whole Brandon thing.

I'll never forgive myself if it's MY fault that he doesn't get his entry in on time and loses out on that opportunity for scholarship money. Just great ☹!!

Since I was feeling a little depressed, I decided to go to the studio to practice my vocals with the music tracks.

I really love my song "DORKS RULE!" And singing it always makes me feel better about my own very dorky, out-of-control life. Especially with all of the drama I've been having lately.

I was at the studio, totally lost in my song, when I got an unexpected visitor. . . .

ME, PRACTICING IN THE STUDIO
WHEN AN UNEXPECTED VISITOR DROPS IN

242

It was BRANDON 😊!!

I was shocked and surprised to see HIM, of all people. He smiled and waved.

As I sang he stared at me through the window. He seemed to be in a serious mood, even a little sad.

After I finished the song, he actually clapped for me and I playfully took a bow.

That's when the most brilliant idea suddenly popped into my head.

"This is PERFECT timing, Brandon!" I said as he entered the booth. "I'm about done here. So let's go across the street to Crazy Burger and work on your project! It'll be MY treat!"

"Actually, that's what I wanted to talk to you about. I'm a little bummed right now about this whole scholarship thing. I guess I just need to vent," Brandon said, shoving his hands into his pockets and staring at the floor.

"I don't blame you. If I were you, I'd be mad at me too! But I can help you right now if—"

"Nikki, I'm NOT mad. Well, not at YOU, anyway. It took a lot of digging, but I was able to get all of your interview info by using material from your TV show and previous newspaper articles. I FINALLY got it done and submitted it to the scholarship committee yesterday."

"Are you serious?! It's DONE?!!" I shrieked in surprise. "That's great news, Brandon!"

It felt like a ton of bricks had suddenly been lifted off my shoulders.

"Congratulations! I'm really happy for you!" I gushed.

"Well, don't be. Unfortunately, I just got an e-mail two hours ago from the committee, saying my entry was rejected! Apparently, someone else had already submitted a project almost identical to mine!"

"NO WAY!!" I gasped in disbelief. "That's impossible!

Yours is about a WCD student working on a once-in-a-lifetime project with Trevor Chase! No one else is doing that but ME! There HAS to be some kind of mistake!"

Brandon shook his head in disgust. "They told me the person's name. I'll give you one guess!" The name came out of my mouth like a foul taste!

"MACKENZIE!!!" I groaned. "Why would she even be applying for a scholarship? Her family is loaded! And why would she steal YOUR topic?"

"Who knows? Maybe because I told her about it. Which I realize now was a stupid thing to do."

I was speechless! And I felt totally responsible.

If Brandon hadn't been wasting time waiting around for me to help him (while I was busy snoozing in the library or fighting with MacKenzie over choreography), he probably would have finished and submitted his entry weeks ago. I blinked back my tears.

BRANDON, TELLING ME THE VERY BAD NEWS
THAT HIS SCHOLARSHIP ENTRY
WAS REJECTED!!

"No, it's not, Nikki! Just because I applied for the scholarship doesn't mean I was actually going to get it. Besides, I can get a summer job at Crazy Burger or even Queasy Cheesy. I know it won't even begin to cover my entire tuition. But every little bit will help! Right?!"

THAT made me feel even WORSE!

"But, Brandon, you spend your summers helping out at Fuzzy Friends! You LOVE that place!"

"I'll just have to find some volunteers to replace me. It's NOT the end of the world!"

I buried my face in my hands and tried to think. "I know! You can start working on a NEW project! Tonight! And I can help by—"

"Nikki, the deadline is this Saturday at midnight. That's just two days! I'd never get it done in time. Plus, we have the listening party at Swanky Hill. After all your hard work, I wouldn't miss that for the world!"

Suddenly I became angry. Not so much at Brandon, but at myself!

"Brandon, don't be so immature! That scholarship is ten times more important than hanging out at some ski resort with your best buds. Besides, I really don't WANT you at the listening party if it's just a convenient excuse for you to give up like this! I don't need that on MY conscience!"

Brandon looked stunned and hurt. I immediately wished I could take back my words. It had ALWAYS been about ME these past few weeks! I had turned into a self-centered, egotistical SNOB! Right before my very own eyes! But Brandon was way too nice to tell me that. Instead, he just shrugged and stared at me. "Whatever, Nikki. I'll think about it, okay? See you later."

I felt just . . . HORRIBLE! "Wait! Brandon, we—"

But that was all I managed to say before he grabbed his coat and walked out the door. WHY did I keep hurting my friend like this ☹?!

A wave of hopelessness washed over me, and my heart actually ached. I sighed deeply and turned on the track to "Dorks Rule!" again. Only, instead of singing my song . . .

I mostly cried through it. ☹!!

I was still pretty upset about Brandon. But today was my last martial arts class, and my main goal was to survive it.

The final exam included a test of skill and a test of knowledge. After totally bombing the Hawk's pop quiz, I knew I had to bust my butt to get a passing grade.

So I had studied before and after school and between reality show filming, voice lessons, band rehearsals, dance practice, and recording at the studio.

Then, just to be on the safe side, I watched all of the Karate Kid movies (again) back-to-back and took notes.

"Today, pip-squeaks, is judgment day!" Sensei Hawk announced dramatically. "You will be put through several rigorous trials and mental challenges. If you have what it takes to complete these tasks, you will become a full-fledged Hawkling. Can you handle the Hawk's epic exam of DOOM?!"

I glanced around the room and everyone was sweating bullets. It looked like I wasn't the ONLY one who had failed that stupid quiz.

"Here's the first part of your challenge. It will test your knowledge," the Hawk said as he passed out the written part of the exam. "You have only fifteen minutes to complete it. You may begin now. If you DARE!"

As I read over the test I started to panic and my mind went completely blank. It didn't help that MacKenzie was glaring at me from across the room.

Finally I closed my eyes and took three deep breaths. I KNEW this stuff. I just needed to FOCUS!

Luckily, I finished the test just as time ran out! The Hawk quickly corrected them as we warmed up for the physical part of our test.

I couldn't believe it, but all my studying really paid off!

THE HAWK'S FINAL EXAM   NAME: Nikki Maxwell

There are many different styles of martial arts. Name at least 8:

1) Kung Fu
2) Karate
3) Jiujitsu
4) Judo

5) Aikido
6) Muay Thai
7) Tai Chi
8) Tae Kwon Do

100%

A+

Name at least 3 for each of the following:

Kicks - front kick, side kick, & roundhouse kick
Blocks - upper block, lower block & outside block
Strikes - palm strike, claw strike & elbow strike
Stances - ready stance, cat stance & long stance

What color belt is the lowest rank, and what does the color represent?

WHITE BELT — the lack of color means the student is a beginner with no knowledge of martial arts. As the student progresses, color belts are awarded based on knowledge and advancement of skills. Typical belt colors by rank are white, yellow, orange, green, blue, purple, brown, red, and black.

Match the following words with their definitions:

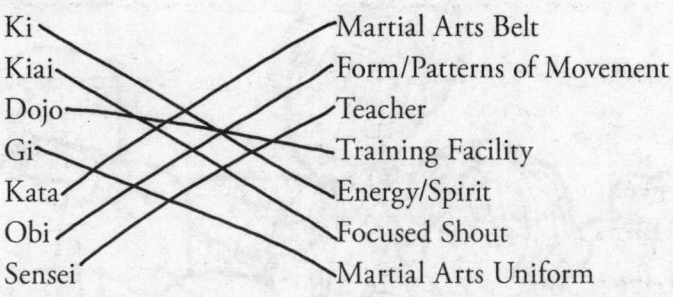

Ki	Martial Arts Belt
Kiai	Form/Patterns of Movement
Dojo	Teacher
Gi	Training Facility
Kata	Energy/Spirit
Obi	Focused Shout
Sensei	Martial Arts Uniform

"Maxwell! Very impressive!" he said to me with a nod of approval. And a mouthful of spaghetti.

The entire class stared in disbelief as a meatball rolled down his chin and bounced off his belly and landed on the gym floor with a *SPLAT.*

The second part of the exam was the physical challenge, and it was definitely rigorous. We had to punch and kick for over thirty minutes!

"I . . . am so *NOT* going to miss this class!" Zoey panted.

"J—just hang in there!" I panted back. "It'll all be over very soon!"

CHLOE, ZOEY, AND ME,
COMPLETING OUR PHYSICAL
TESTING IN MARTIAL ARTS CLASS

"UGH! . . ." Chloe looked around for our teacher. "I don't think it'll be over anytime soon, guys! Turkey leg at six o'clock!"

She pointed at Sensei Hawkins sitting on the bleachers with a giant turkey leg in his mouth.

"Oh, that's just terrific!" Zoey stopped punching and groaned. "Nikki, I normally don't condone violence. But PLEASE sucker punch him again! And put an end to this MADNESS!"

"Shhhh! Just calm down, Zoey!" I said. "You know I can't do that!"

"SENSEI HAWKINS!" MacKenzie screamed. "My armpits are getting sweaty and my curls are going flat! We have to stop NOW!"

Sensei tossed the turkey leg bone over his shoulder and took one last slurp from his supersize soda.

Then he looked at the clock.

"Time is up! Please stop. The Hawk's meal, er, I mean, intense TESTING is finally complete," he announced. "Please line up!"

Chloe, Zoey, and I were so exhausted we could barely walk. Somehow, we managed to stagger to our place in line.

"CONGRATULATIONS! You have all completed the second challenge! Let the Hawkling Award Ceremony commence!" he said proudly.

I have to admit, the Hawk's teaching methods are very creative and a little weird. And so are the yellow karate belts he gave us.

They are covered in shiny glitter and sequins to, as he put it, "blind your enemies with jealousy!" At least he got the BLINDING part right. But I'm not complaining! I'm SUPERproud of the belt he gave me.

It has sparkly fake diamonds that spell out "Most Improved."

OMG! I never would have thought I'd actually win a martial arts award!

CHLOE, ZOEY, AND I SUCCESSFULLY
EARN OUR YELLOW BELTS!!

"May the claw be with you, Hawklings! You're welcome to train at my dojo anytime." Then the Hawk bowed to us. "Sayonara!"

After spending almost a month with the crazy guy, I was a little sad to see him go.

I'm really going to miss the narcissism, the way he yelled at us, and that never-ending supply of food that he somehow kept stuffed in his shirt.

Who knows? One day I just might pay his dojo a visit.

But enough of that sentimental sissy talk! Hawklings don't shed tears! Hey, I'M so TOUGH, I make my TEARS cry!

HIII-YIAAA!!

Now I just need to find a sixteen-piece bucket of chicken wing-dings to snack on!

!!

SATURDAY, MARCH 29

Today was finally the day of our "Dorks Rule!" listening party at Swanky Hill Ski Resort!

Even though I felt bad about Brandon possibly missing out, I was looking forward to actually seeing the place I'd heard so much about from the kids at school. MacKenzie and all of the CCP girls were planning to have their sweet sixteen birthday parties there.

As a special surprise and a reward for all of my hard work, Trevor Chase booked a VIP suite for an overnight stay for my family and me!

He'd also arranged for us to be picked up and transported by a limo service! YES! We were actually riding to Swanky Hill in a limo like REAL celebrities! SQUEEEE!!!

After arriving, we are going to have a special breakfast prepared by a private chef right in our suite!

Then we were going to spend the ENTIRE day hanging out on the slopes, relaxing in the spa, and lounging around the pool. It's going to be FABULICIOUS!

And later that evening, at 7:00 p.m., I'd be meeting up with my band members in the convention center for our listening party.

Due to the popularity of the TV show, we were expecting twenty busloads of fans from neighboring schools, in addition to those arriving by car.

The first one thousand people would be able to buy a copy of our "Dorks Rule!" CD ten days early.

I couldn't contain my excitement when the iron gates opened and we traveled on a private drive up this huge snow—covered mountain.

Then, tucked inside a grove of evergreen trees, was the entrance to Swanky Hill.

"OMG! Just look at this place! SWEET!!" I gushed. . . .

MY FAMILY AND ME, ARRIVING BY LIMO AT
SWANKY HILL SKI RESORT!!

Swanky Hill isn't an ordinary, run-of-the-mill family ski resort. It is known for its luxurious facilities, five-star restaurants, to-die-for spa treatments, first-class country club, convention center, and even celebrity sightings.

And today, in addition to our special event, it was hosting the Extreme Ski Championship!

It's a competition where crazy young people ski down slopes, dodging trees and boulders, and doing double flips off of cliffs. How COOL is THAT? ☺!!

So the resort was crowded with spectators, tourists, and skiers.

While we were checking in, the resort clerk asked if we wanted to use their designer ski apparel and equipment because it was all FREE with our VIP reservations.

OMG! It was like being at a large ski boutique in the mall or something. The stuff was beyond GORGEOUS! It was SWANKY!!

But my dad told her no thanks! He said that we were all set because he and my mom had pretty much MADE everything we needed.

Okay! That's when I started to get ~~a little~~ REALLY worried.

Mainly because "normal" people don't "make" ski apparel and equipment. Especially if they're VIP celeb guests at Swanky Hill for a listening party.

OMG! When I first saw our ski gear, I could barely stand to look at it. It was just THAT ugly! But mostly I couldn't look because the bright yellow fluorescent color was almost blinding.

But the weirdest thing was that all the gear looked vaguely familiar. Suddenly I remembered where I'd seen all of it before.

Last summer I went with Dad to the annual City Hall Rummage Sale, where the various departments sell off excess and unwanted uniforms, equipment, supplies, and other items.

Dad thought he'd hit the jackpot when he stumbled upon some fluorescent yellow glow-in-the-dark winter sanitation suits that the city garbage workers hated and were trying to get rid of.

And when he saw the large sign above them that said FREE! PLEASE TAKE AS MANY AS YOU CAN CARRY!! he went crazy and grabbed one for every member of our family.

He also snagged some used wool hats, sanitation goggles, and hazmat boots and gloves that were only $1.00 each.

Dad had started this fiasco, but it was quite obvious that Mom had finished it—as one massive craft project.

She had decorated our ~~sanitation~~ snowsuits by adding red velvet hearts to the pockets, elbows, and knees, and plastic-jeweled heart trim down the legs and arms. Our hats and ~~hazmat~~ ski boots, gloves, and goggles were trimmed with red hearts as well.

OMG! We looked totally RIDONKULOUS!

266

I pleaded with Dad to let me change into the snazzy designer stuff from the resort so I'd fit in with all of the other skiers.

He insisted that we wear our homemade ski outfits, since Mom had poured so much love into decorating them. But we DID get to use the resort's helmets, boots, and skis.

When we went on the ski lifts, everyone just stopped and STARED at us in AWE!

And not because our suits were SUPERugly. Which they were.

People were gawking because our snowsuits were such a freakishly BRIGHT YELLOW that they mistakenly thought we were the SUNRISE! Even though it was almost noon.

OMG! I thought I was going to DIE of EMBARRASSMENT dangling a thousand feet in the air. . . .

PEOPLE STARING AT US ON THE SKI LIFT
AND MISTAKING US FOR THE SUNRISE!!

And Brianna didn't have a CLUE!

She was actually smiling, waving, and blowing kisses to everyone like she was a contestant on *Toddlers & Tiaras* or somebody.

But I guess things could have been a lot worse! Thank goodness Dad didn't purchase those buy-one-get-one-free bright orange jumpsuits that came complete with serial numbers, flip-flops, handcuffs, and leg shackles from the county jail.

Instead of sanitation workers, we'd look like a family of thuggish PRISON ESCAPEES!

Anyway, since Brianna and I had never skied before, Mom suggested that we both start at the bunny hill, which is for beginners.

I was really excited about finally learning how to ski. And Brianna was really excited about meeting the BUNNY (don't ask)! But it was a total bummer being in a class with three- to six-year-olds.

Brianna must have been embarrassed too, because she pretended like she didn't know me and kept calling me "Hey, you!" . . .

ME, ACCIDENTALLY RUNNING
INTO ANOTHER LITTLE KID

But I couldn't help it! Whenever my skis would go crooked, I'd lose control.

Anyway, after about an hour, I was starting to get the hang of things. And finally I could make it down the bunny hill without falling.

Or knocking over any little kids. **Woo-hoo!**

That's when I noticed this really sweet ski outfit with a coordinating shearling headband.

It wasn't the typical stuff you'd find at a store. It was a designer, goose down, high-performance suit you'd see on the cover of a pro ski magazine.

As I was trying to get a closer look, the person slowly turned around and stared at me with her icy-cold blue eyes!

OMG! It was MACKENZIE ☹!

I was so shocked to see HER there, I almost threw up my breakfast right on her designer ski boots.

271

Had she actually come to Swanky Hill to attend our listening party?!! Especially after she'd . . .

1. thrown that big hissy fit about me missing a dance practice last week

2. threatened to report me to Trevor Chase

AND

3. spread all of those malicious lies about me on camera!!

MacKenzie glared at me with this condescending smirk and eyeballed me from head to toe.

"OMG, Nikki! So that was YOUR family in those hideously tacky ski outfits! You guys look like city garbage workers. Trash pickup at this resort is on Monday, not today." MacKenzie cackled like a witch.

How dare that girl insult my family right to my FACE like that?!!!

Okay! So maybe MacKenzie was right.

We WERE dressed like city garbage workers.

But STILL!

Our personal wardrobe choices were none of her ding-dang business.

Sorry, but I was SO sick of her STANK attitude!

Right then I wanted to SCREAM . . . at the top of my lungs . . . for the . . . abominable snow creature . . . to come rushing down from the mountaintop and . . . snatch MacKenzie by her . . . lovely hair and . . . drag her off . . . to be his . . . um, PERSONAL POOPER-SCOOPER . . . for the rest of her PATHETIC little life!

But no such luck ☹!

"Very funny, MacKenzie! But we're NOT garbage

workers. And just in case you've forgotten, Chloe, Zoey, Violet, Marcus, Theo, and I have a televised listening party later this evening," I said, gritting my teeth.

Suddenly she stared at me with a quizzical look on her face and smirked. "Oh, really? Well, I hope you don't mind me asking a personal question, but . . ."

I just knew she was going to make a big deal about Brandon possibly NOT being here to support me and the band at such an important event.

It wasn't that he didn't CARE!

I had insisted that he NOT come.

His scholarship was way more important than him being the drummer in our band.

She glared at me and then asked a very probing question that was none of her business. . . .

MACKENZIE, ASKING ME
ABOUT THE BUNNY SLOPE

"Who, ME?! Of course NOT! I'm just here . . . um . . . teaching my little sister to ski. Actually!"

"Oh really?" she said, eyeballing me like I was lying to her or something.

"Really! I've been downhill skiing at, um . . . Dead Man's Drop for years!"

"Dead Man's—? Wait a minute! Isn't that the name of the hill my little sister and her friends sled on?"

"Of course NOT! It's a totally different place. I'm talking about Dead Man's Drop luxury ski resort! It's the playground of the rich and famous. It's even SWANKIER than Swanky Hill," I lied. "It makes THIS place look like a dump! Actually."

"Yeah right, Nikki! Just tell the truth! I know why you're really out here on the ski slopes today!"

"You D-DO?!" I sputtered, wondering how she'd found out Trevor had paid for my family to stay at Swanky Hill! Holiday Inn was a big splurge for us.

We couldn't afford this place in a million years!

"If you're a downhill skier, then you're obviously out here to see the Extreme Ski Competition. Especially since BRANDON is covering it for the school newspaper. Come on, I'm NOT stupid!"

"Okay! Yes. I AM here for that ski thingy. Actually," I lied again. "And Brandon's really covering it? Yep. I knew THAT too!"

"Well, I have to go. I'm NOT a spectator like you. I'm actually competing. So wish me luck! Loser!" MacKenzie cackled as she shushed away.

That's when I decided to ditch the bunny hill and dump Brianna with my parents. It was more important for me to try to talk to Brandon and clear the air. That is, IF he actually showed up.

By the time I took the ski lift to the top of Paranoid Peak, the competition was just starting for the middle school division. I expected MacKenzie to be good, and she was. . . .

MACKENZIE, SPEEDING DOWN THE
SKI JUMP AND LANDING A
BREATHTAKING DOUBLE FLIP!!

I hated to admit it, but MacKenzie was better than good. She was AWESOME!! All of the spectators cheered for her, and she smiled and waved.

I wasn't surprised that she got the highest score for our age group: 8.7 out of 10.

When MacKenzie came back to pick up her gear, I warmly congratulated her. But she totally ignored me and high-fived all of her CCP friends. And yes! I felt like a stupid outcast ☹!

That's when I suddenly noticed a cute guy in a familiar blue jacket taking photos of the skiers at the bottom of the hill.

OMG! It was BRANDON!

Apparently, he had decided to hang out at Swanky Hill after all. Against my advice.

I shouted his name and waved, but he didn't hear me. So I very carefully scooted to the edge of the ski ramp and called him again. "BRAAANDON!!"

Finally he heard me. A big smile flashed across his face, and he waved and yelled, "HI, NIKKI! SMILE!"

BRANDON AND ME, SPOTTING EACH OTHER IN THE CROWD AND WAVING

Then suddenly somebody PUSHED ME!!

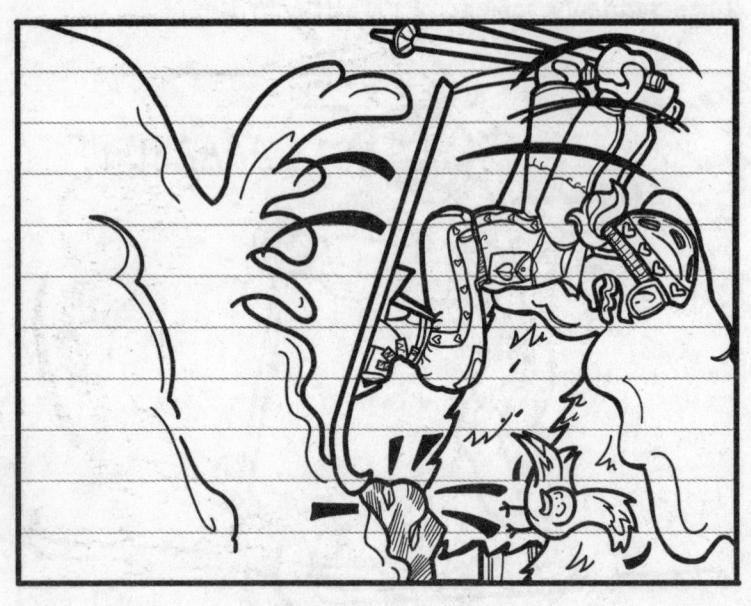

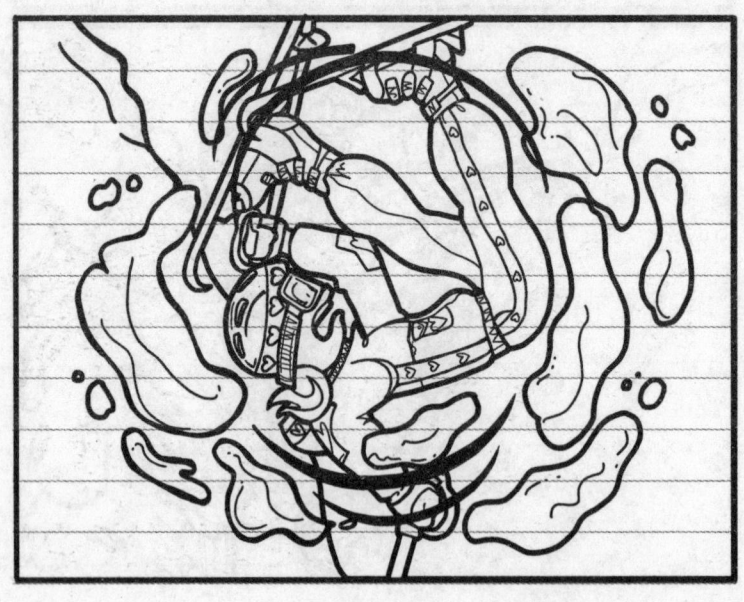

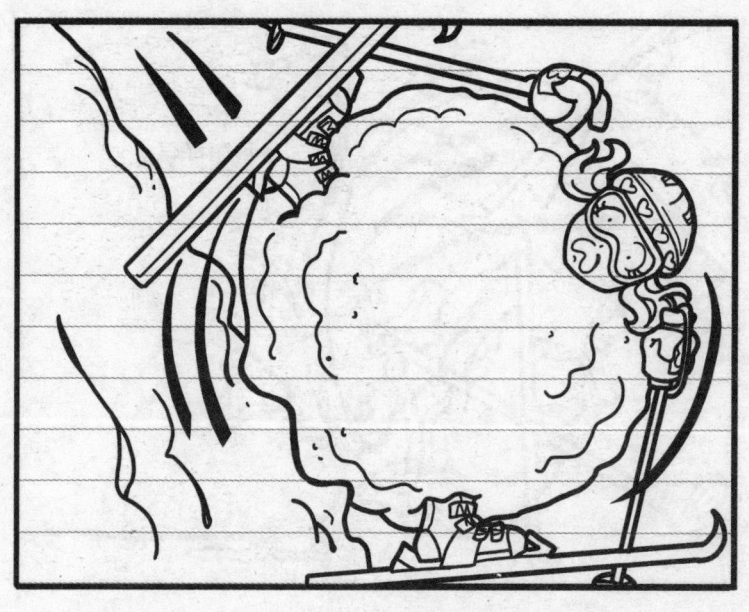

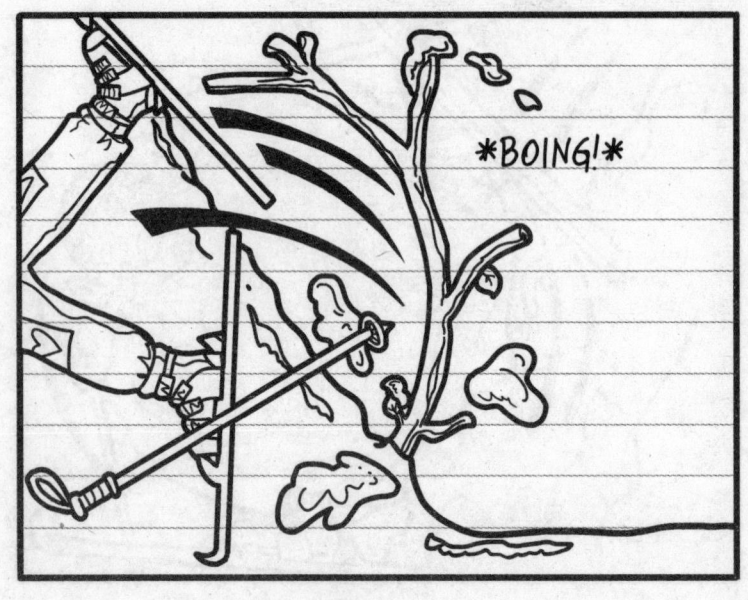

284

OMG! On the way down the slope, I . . .

1. hit a boulder

2. did three front somersaults

3. smashed into a tree

4. did a double backflip

5. did two aerial cartwheels

6. lost my ski poles, and then

7. . . . AAAAAAAHHHH!!!

As a skier, I was EXTREMELY . . . AWFUL ☹! But lucky for me, it was an EXTREME Ski Competition.

I was actually a SUPERclumsy beginner, barely able to make it down the bunny hill. But the judges thought I was a SUPERgutsy daredevil.

And this is the KA-RAY-ZEE part!!

I LANDED HEADFIRST IN A SNOWBANK,
SCORED A PERFECT 10, AND WON FIRST PLACE!

SQUEEEE 😊!! MacKenzie came in second place, and she was NOT happy. Sorry, MacKenzie! But that's what you get for pushing me off that ski jump!

BRANDON TOOK LOTS OF PICTURES!

Including one of me and my family posing with my new trophy. I had to admit, we looked SUPERcool in our FUNKY homemade ski gear. . . .

OMG! People were begging to know where we got all of our "designer" skiwear and equipment!

But it was OUR little secret ☺!!

After all of the excitement, Brandon and I decided to hang out inside the resort. We found a SUPERcozy spot to talk and sipped on steaming mugs of hot chocolate with whipped cream and marshmallows. YUM!!

Although I was happy to see him, I still felt really bad about that fight we'd had at the recording studio. And deep down, I couldn't shake the feeling that it was mostly my fault that his scholarship entry had been rejected.

It was quite obvious. After Brandon had chosen to write about me, MacKenzie, in a jealous rage, had retaliated by stealing his topic and competing against him. Then she had manipulated my schedule to make it nearly impossible for Brandon and me to get his entry finished and submitted on time. I hated to admit it, but the girl was an EVIL GENIUS!!

Suddenly I noticed Brandon was really quiet and seemed totally lost in thought, like me. We just sat there kind of staring at each other. Can you say AWKWARD?

Finally I cleared my throat. "So, um, what did you decide to do about your scholarship entry?"

"I stayed up most of the night trying to come up with another idea, but it was hopeless. It took me practically three weeks to complete my first entry. So there's no way I can do a new one in just a day or two," he explained sadly.

"But what about your tuition?!" I asked, trying to swallow the huge lump in my throat.

"I—I don't know," Brandon stammered. "I'm actually considering transferring to another school. But we could still be friends and hang out. Right?!"

I felt like I'd just been punched in the stomach.

BRANDON WAS LEAVING WCD??!! ☹!!

"NOOOOOOOOO!!!!!" I screamed inside my head as I blinked back tears.

"You might TRANSFER?!" I croaked in shock.

He stared at the floor, sighed, and nodded. "I don't want to, but I really don't have a choice. After I gave up on the scholarship entry, I figured I might as well hang out at Swanky Hill and attend our listening party with friends. Plus, I had volunteered to cover the Extreme Ski Competition for the school newspaper since I was going to be here."

His gloomy expression faded slightly as he browsed through the photos on his digital camera. "Wow! Just look at these photos. I had no idea you were a skier! And why didn't you tell me you were competing today? I was really surprised."

"Yeah, I was REALLY surprised too. You have no idea! The whole thing was totally unplanned."

Then he showed me all of the action shots he'd taken of me during the Extreme Ski Competition.

I told him his photos were AWESOME and he was a SUPERtalented photographer. Then he told me I was an AWESOME skier. That's when it occurred to me that between MY skiing and HIS photography, we made an AWESOME team!

A wave of sadness washed over me. OMG! I was going to miss him SO much if he transferred to another school ☹!!

"So, Brandon, um . . . you'll at least finish out the year at WCD, right?" I asked, dreading his answer.

"I'm not sure. There's a big meeting with Principal Winston next Thursday," he answered glumly.

Then we just sat there, staring at each other and feeling hopeless. It was almost like we were already missing each other. I think both of us were trying to keep from crying. Probably. That's when I suddenly got the most brilliant idea. I started laughing really loud, like an insane person.

Brandon was totally confused. "What's so funny?!"

He grabbed the school newspaper's iPad and within minutes had e-mailed in a new entry. Then he brushed his shaggy bangs out of his eyes and gave me this huge smile. I blushed profusely (although I had a really CREEPY feeling someone was watching us).

WE SAT IN FRONT OF THE FIRE,
SMILING, BLUSHING, AND FLIRTING
WITH EACH OTHER, LIKE, FOREVER!!

Before we knew it, our listening party was starting in less than an hour. So I told Brandon I'd see him later and ran up to my suite to get dressed.

I was even more excited about the listening party now that Brandon was going to be participating ☺!

As much as I enjoyed the celebrity of having my own camera crew following me around and studio recording sessions with some of the best producers in the industry, I was really looking forward to just going back to being plain ol' ME!

Tonight I was going to be filming the very last episode of my reality show. And to be honest, I was SUPERrelieved it was finally almost over. I'd had some fun and exciting moments. But mostly it was stressful, intense, and exhausting.

I don't even remember the last time I went to bed before midnight or slept past 6:00 a.m.

Yes, this past month of my life has been SUPERglamorous. But I've had little or no time for my classes, my homework, my family, my BFFs, Brandon, and most important, ME!

I took the elevator from our VIP suite down to the convention center. At the main entrance, I could see that everything was already set up. Off to the right, crews were rushing around setting up equipment for the television and radio stations that would be covering the event live.

The Kidz Rockin' performers were on a large stage on the left, running through a quick dress rehearsal.

The air was filled with the yummy-smelling aroma of a dozen food booths selling everything from cotton candy to hot dogs to elephant ears. Right in the heart of the festivities at center court was a large area cordoned off by velvet ropes.

There was a humongous banner hanging from the ceiling with our band's photo and name on it.

OMG! It appeared to be at least half a block long. I gulped and immediately felt overwhelmed. . . .

ME, ADMIRING THE HUGE BANNER
OF US HANGING FROM THE CEILING!

I found a seat with my name on it at the long table where we'd be signing autographs and meeting fans.

A series of ten-foot-tall speakers set up in the area would be blasting our music during the event.

One thing was for sure: Trevor Chase and his team had spared no expense to make sure that our listening party was a humongous success.

I just hoped everyone actually liked our music. And US, for that matter!

When Chloe, Zoey, and Violet finally arrived, they came in with their necks craned, staring up at the huge banner overhead just like I had.

We did a group hug and giggled with excitement.

Soon after, the guys arrived with two hotel security guards, each pushing a cart stacked high with boxes of our CDs.

As the guards piled the boxes under the tables, we all chatted with each other and tried to calm our nerves.

I couldn't believe that people were already starting to line up outside the velvet ropes for our meet and greet.

We sat and watched in awe as the line grew longer and longer.

Soon a dozen or so security guards were stationed at posts nearby to help manage the crowd.

Our director rushed up to us, talking a mile a minute. "Can you believe this crowd?! They're all here for you guys! I think we're going to sell out! The live telecast will be starting in ten minutes! So let's get these boxes of CDs opened so we'll be ready to rock!"

We each grabbed a box, tore it open, and just stared inside in shock.

Other than paper and packing materials, they were completely empty!

I felt like I had been punched in the stomach!

All I could do was blink in disbelief and hope that my eyes were playing tricks on me.

"What happened to our CDs?" Chloe screeched.

"OMG! Nikki, what are we going to do?" Zoey moaned.

"Obviously, there's been some kind of mix—up," Brandon said, shaking his head.

I glanced at the noisy, impatient crowd that had swelled to what looked like a thousand people. And they were chanting our name. Just GREAT ☹!!

Trevor Chase was going to fire us and then sue for all of the money he'd lost. Our listening party was pretty much ruined!

The director ran up to us again. "We go live in three minutes!" she exclaimed excitedly. "Take your places, please!"

I'd almost forgotten the worst of it. We were about to be publicly humiliated LIVE on television ☹.

MacKenzie was probably gleefully watching this train wreck from the crowd with a big box of popcorn.

Right then I wanted to run to the nearest bathroom, lock myself in a stall, and NEVER come out.

Brandon stared at the growing crowd and chewed his lip nervously. "So, um, what are we going to do? Any ideas?" he asked, drumming his fingers on the table.

"I was considering just canceling the whole thing. But I think it's a little late!!"

"Yeah, kind of!" Brandon smiled weakly. "But I'm sure you'll think of something. You always do!"

"Well, none of that will matter when this angry mob tears us to shreds when we tell them there are no CDs to buy and they can just go home!" I muttered.

"Kidz Rockin' really needs this money, and I've let them down. I just feel like such a . . . LOSER!" I said, blinking back tears.

"Nikki, it wasn't your fault! Somehow the boxes just got mixed up or something!"

"Yeah, MacKenzie strikes again! She ruined our first kiss, and now our listening party!" I fumed.

OMG! Did I just say that out loud?

Yes, I think I DID.

I cringed and stared at the floor in embarrassment.

Brandon looked a little surprised and grinned. "Why are you thinking about THAT at a time like this?!" he teased.

Of course I blushed and rolled my eyes. And he blushed and gave me a big warm smile. The way we were flirting, you wouldn't have believed a riot was going to be breaking out any minute now!

"Sixty seconds to airtime!" our director announced. "Nikki, you'll be addressing the fans right after the band is introduced, just like we discussed. The mic right in front of you will be on. Good luck! Places, please."

Chloe, Zoey, and I did a group hug.

Guys, I'm so sorry I screwed this up. Ultimately, I'm responsible. I should have checked those boxes before they left the studio.

That's when Zoey squeezed my hand and said, "A life spent making mistakes is not only more honorable, but more useful than a life spent doing nothing.—George Bernard Shaw."

"Well, whatever happens, we've got your back, girlfriend! Unless, of course, the crowd gets mad and decides to tar and feather us. Then I'll be leaving you in the dust!" Chloe joked, and gave me jazz hands.

While we were being introduced by the mayor, I completely zoned out and didn't hear a word he was saying. I was busy trying to figure out what I was going to say to over a thousand people who had turned out to support our band and the charity Kidz Rockin'!

Well, one thing was for sure—we could KISS our music careers good-bye!

UGH! There was that four-letter word again!

That's when the craziest idea popped into my head!

We didn't have any CDs to sell for charity. But maybe we had something else. And if our fans really, really liked us, they might be willing to buy THAT instead.

I quickly jotted my idea down and passed the note to Chloe and Zoey!

Crazy idea! Let's do a KISSING BOOTH!

They both looked mortified at first. But after talking it over together, they finally agreed.

Then they passed the note on to everyone else.

Violet gave me a big smile and a thumbs-up.

Theo and Marcus both blushed profusely and then nodded.

And Brandon just laughed and shook his head.

Then he made a circular motion with his finger at the side of his head, which meant that I was KA-RAY-ZEE!

Hey, people!

Desperate times call for desperate measures!

By that time, the mayor was just finishing up his welcome speech.

"It is with great pride that I introduce a talented future pop star and TV star, Nikki Maxwell, with her band, um . . . . Actually, I'm Not Really Sure Yet?!"

The crowd went wild! They clapped and screamed in excitement for, like, two whole minutes.

I guess they really DID like us!

When they finally quieted down, I started by thanking everyone for coming to our listening party and for supporting our fund-raiser for Kidz Rockin'. . . .

Then I took a deep breath and continued. "But before we get started with our meet and greet, I have a special announcement I'd like to make. We had originally planned to sell our CDs and donate the proceeds to Kidz Rockin'! But soon you'll be able to get the CD everywhere. This is our hometown, and we think you all deserve something even more exciting and special! What do you guys think?"

The crowd went wild again.

"So to help raise funds for Kidz Rockin', tonight we're accepting donations for HUGS and KISSES from your favorite band member. How does that sound?!"

The crowd loved the idea! They cheered more excitedly than ever. So for the next three hours, we met with fans, signed autographs, and posed for photos.

And YES! We sold hugs for $3.00 and kisses (on the cheek) for $5.00 from your favorite band member.

All for a great cause—the Kidz Rockin' charity. And OMG! It was a BLAST!

And a lot of fans came back for seconds! And even thirds!

By the end of the night, we had raised over $8,000 for some VERY deserving kids. . . .

MY BAND, POSING WITH THE
CUTE LITTLE KIDS FROM KIDZ ROCKIN'!!

I was SO happy ☺!

SQUEEEE!

But more than anything, I was really proud of my friends Chloe, Zoey, Violet, Theo, Marcus, and Brandon for agreeing to do all of this after our CDs went missing.

Just as we were finishing up, I noticed Brandon kind of staring at me. Then he left his seat and got in line at the table!

MY line! I just rolled my eyes at him. That guy was such a PRANKSTER!

"Nice to meet you. Would YOU like my autograph? And how about a photo, too?" I teased.

"Actually, I'd personally like to make a donation to Kidz Rockin'!" he said, and handed me $5.00.

At first I just kind of stared at him, confused. Then suddenly everything made perfect sense.

I realized that Brandon was paying $5.00 because he wanted to buy a KISS!! From ME?!!!!!!

I was like, OMG! OMG! OMG!

Was he actually SERIOUS?!

I thought I was going to PEE my PANTS right there on the spot!

He just stood there, holding the $5.00, waiting for me to take it. So finally I took it from him.

And you'd NEVER believe what happened next . . . !!!

OMG! I can't believe it's almost 1:00 a.m.!! I've been writing this entry, like, FOREVER! Sorry, but I'm SO exhausted, I can barely keep my eyes open. I'll finish this entry later. Maybe . . . !!

I know! I'm SUCH a DORK! GOOD NIGHT!

Okay. This is LATER. . . .

NIKKI MAXWELL:
THE MAKING OF A POP PRINCESS!
EPISODE #8

MY FIRST KISS!

MacKenzie is still supermad at me because I beat her in the Extreme Ski Competition on Saturday.

And get this! She totally ignored me at my locker this morning when I tried to congratulate her on her second-place finish.

Hey, I was just trying to be friendly and show good sportsmanship.

NOT! ☺!

Actually, I was trying to RUB HER NOSE in the fact that I'd given her a good BEATDOWN on the ski slopes at Swanky Hill Ski Resort!

Anyway, I'm supposed to be sitting here in class conjugating French verbs.

But HOW in the world am I supposed to concentrate on something as boringly mundane as conjugating French verbs when Brandon kissed me?!

OMG! BRANDON ACTUALLY KISSED ME!

YES!! He. Kissed. ME!

SQUEEEEEEE!

He is such a sweetheart to do that for charity ☺!!

Wait a minute! Oh, CRUD!! NOOOOO!!!!

IF it was for charity, maybe he didn't mean for it to be a REAL kiss?! ☹!! But only a kiss to, like, help needy children?!

Which is GOOD for them. But BAD for ME!! Because that means we're just two very good friends helping to make the world a better place. Which is wonderful! And horrible at the same time!

JUST GREAT!! ☹!

Now I'm REALLY confused!!

WHICH kind of kiss was it?!

A just-a-friend kiss?

A let's-save-the-world kiss?

Or a you're-my-girlfriend kiss?

I could just ask him. But then he'd think that I thought it was a really big deal.

And I DO! But I don't want HIM to know that!

SORRY!

I can't help it.

I'm SUCH a DORK!!

☺!!

Mirror Mirror on the wall, who is the dorkiest princess of them all?

Cinderella? ← —— No

Uh uh —→ Sleeping Beauty?

Yes! . . .

Nikki Maxwell? ← —— Wait . . . What?!

Will Nikki find her happily ever after, or will it be an epic fairy fail for this dorkarella? Find out in *ONCE UPON A DORK...*

GOOD WITCH OF THE
NORTH'S HOUSE

QUEEN OF
HEARTS' CASTLE

FAIRY
HEADQUARTERS

WICKED WITCH
OF THE WEST'S
HOUSE

AAAAAAAAAAHHH ☹!!
(That was me screaming in frustration!)

I can't believe I overslept! AGAIN! Now I'm probably going to be late for school! WHY?!! Because my bratty little sister, Brianna, has been sneaking into my bedroom at night and stealing my alarm clock!

She's been using it to get up extra early to make a peanut butter, jelly, and pickle sandwich to take to school for lunch. YES! She actually adds PICKLES!

I don't know which is more NAUSEATING, Brianna or her disgusting sandwich!

Anyway, now I have less than three minutes to shower, shampoo, brush, dress, pack, eat, gloss, and GO!

This is how my very CRUDDY day began. . . .

329

HOP!
HOP!

<u>OMG!!</u> I got dressed for school in two minutes and nineteen seconds! Which is probably a NEW late-for-school world record!!

I decided to wear my brand-new sweater with the cool fringe on it. It took me TWO whole months to save up to buy it from SWEET 16, a trendy teen store in the mall.

Looking back on my morning, there was definitely GOOD NEWS and BAD NEWS.

The GOOD NEWS . . . ?

My day had gotten off to such a HORRIBLE start, I was absolutely SURE there was NO WAY things could get any WORSE ☺!

The BAD NEWS . . . ?

I was TOTALLY WRONG about the GOOD NEWS!

!!

OMG! I was so TICKED OFF at Brianna for swiping my alarm clock that smoke was practically spewing out of my EARS!! . . .

I wanted to stuff her in a big box and ship her off to Princess Sugar Plum Island to be the pooper-scooper for all those cute little baby unicorns she loves so much.

"Brianna! Did you take my clock again?!" I yelled. "If I'M late for school, it's all YOUR fault!"

"I didn't take your clock. Miss Penelope did! She thinks you need all the BEAUTY SLEEP you can get! Have you looked in the mirror lately?" Brianna said, sticking her tongue out at me.

"Miss Penelope THINKS I need beauty sleep?! Sorry, Brianna, but Miss Penelope CAN'T think. She doesn't have a BRAIN! She's a hand puppet!" I shot back.

"She does TOO have a brain!" Brianna shouted. "She says she can go to puppet school to get smarter, but YOU need to go on that TV show *Ugly Face Intervention!*"

I was like, Oh. No. She. DIDN'T ☹!!! I could NOT believe Miss Penelope was talking TRASH about me like that. SHE was going to need an intervention!! After I took a pen and drew her a mustache. THEN we'd see whose FACE was the most messed up, MINE or HERS!

Anyway, Brianna was at the kitchen table, slopping together peanut butter, jelly, and pickles to make her very disgusting sandwich. . . .

BRIANNA, BUSY MAKING
A DISGUSTING PBJ & P SANDWICH!

"Would you like me to make one for you, Nikki? It's yummy! SEE?" Brianna said, shoving her sandwich right in my face.

I cringed at the slimy, drippy mess. . . .

EWW! It SMELLED even worse than it looked. Kind of like peanut butter, jelly, and, um . . . rancid pickle juice ☹!

"Um . . . no thanks!" I muttered, totally grossed out.

"Come on. Just take one bite!!" Brianna said, waving it under my nose. "You'll LOVE it!"

"No, Brianna! Actually, I'm not hungry anymore! I took one look at your sandwich and COMPLETELY lost my appetite!!"

"Are you SURE? It's awesomely delicious!" She giggled.

I just rolled my eyes at that girl.

What part of the word "NO" did she NOT understand?!

I wanted to scream, Sorry, Brianna, but . . .

I will not eat it with a DOG!
I will not eat it with a FROG!

I will not eat it with a CAT!
I will not eat it with a RAT!

I will not eat it in my ROOM.
On the BUS. Or on the MOON!

I will not eat it NORTH or SOUTH!
It made me throw up in my MOUTH!

Call me PICKY! Call me FICKLE!
I DON'T like PBJ and PICKLES ☹!!!

Anyway, Brianna went to the fridge to get a juice box, and I gathered my stuff and was about to head out the door, when suddenly she came charging at me like an angry baby rhinoceros in pigtails.

SHE actually accused ME of taking her sandwich!

That's when we started yelling at each other. . . .

BRIANNA, ACCUSING ME OF SWIPING HER
YUCK-A-LICIOUS SANDWICH!!

"My sandwich is missing, and YOU took it!"

"Brianna! I wouldn't feed that nasty sandwich to my WORST ENEMY!"

And by worst enemy, I meant people like . . . well, you know . . .

MACKENZIE HOLLISTER ☹!!

Although, now that I think about it, I probably WOULD feed that sandwich to my worst enemy.

I'd LOVE to just shove it right down her throat!

Just kidding ☺!

NOT ☹!!

Actually, I really am kidding ☺!

I try to be friendly and get along with EVERYONE at my school. But for some reason, MacKenzie HATES MY GUTS!!

Anyway, by the time I finally left for school, Brianna was busy making another sandwich.

It's like, the older she gets, the more BRATTY she becomes.

I think it's time for me to have a very serious talk with my mom and dad about their parenting skills.

WHY?

Because I'm really SICK and TIRED of Brianna . . .

1. taking my stuff without permission (like my clock!).

2. stealing my cell phone to play the Princess Sugar Plum games and running down my battery.

3. waking me up in the middle of the night to take her to the bathroom, by jumping up and down on my bed (while I'm still in it ☹!!). . . .

BRIANNA, WAKING ME UP
IN A VERY RUDE MANNER!!

It's absolutely vital that my parents get professional help for Brianna before it's too late.

They let her get away with EVERYTHING! But when I ask to do stuff, it's always a big fat "NO!"

I was really looking forward to volunteering at the Fuzzy Friends Animal Rescue Center after school today with my crush, Brandon.

But my mom said I couldn't!

WHY?!! Because I have to babysit BRIANNA!

TYPICAL ☹!!

It was kind of a big deal because this would have been my first time hanging out with Brandon since . . . well, you know!!

My very first KISS!!! SQUEEEEEEEE!!! ☺!!

OMG! I was SO shocked when it happened! I thought I was going to DIE!

It was SO romantic!

Even though my eyes were open the entire time and practically bulging out of my head.

And after it was over, I hyperventilated!

Almost.

The only problem with the kiss is that it happened at a charity event to raise money for kids. So I don't know if Brandon did it because he actually likes me, or because he was just trying to save the needy children of the world.

Anyway, thanks to my KA-RAY-ZEE sister, I'm a nervous wreck and totally stressed out.

And my school day hasn't even started yet!

NOTE TO SELF: Get a NEW sister!!

!!

I was happy and relieved that I actually made it to school on time.

In spite of my very cruddy morning, I'd made up my mind that I was going to have a really good day.

I was surprised that my new sweater got SO much attention.

As I was walking down the hall, practically EVERYONE stopped and stared. Even the GUYS!

And get this!! A few of the CCP (Cute, Cool & Popular) girls actually smiled, pointed, and whispered to each other.

It was quite obvious they were LOVING my new sweater!

I felt just like a fashion model walking the runway or something. . . .

EVERYONE STARING AND POINTING AS
I STRUTTED DOWN THE HALL

I was like, "Good morning, people! Please don't HATE on my FABULOUS sweater!!" But I just said that inside my head, so no one heard it but me.

When I got to my locker, I put my stuff away and was about to write a quick entry in my diary.

I was feeling REALLY happy about my life right then ☺!

I wasn't even that mad at Brianna anymore. Hey, she's ONLY a little kid! When I was her age, I was WAY more annoying.

Suddenly I noticed MacKenzie staring at me like I was a . . . two-headed, um . . . SQUIRREL or something. But I just ignored her like I always do.

Then she shrieked, "OMG, NIKKI! WHERE DID YOU GET THAT SWEATER?!!"

Which was the STUPIDEST question EVER! That girl has the IQ of a wad of chewed bubble gum! . . .

MACKENZIE

WAD OF GUM

I just glared at her and calmly answered, "I got my sweater from a STORE. You know, where YOU buy stuff, like your HAIR and your TAN."

MacKenzie was obviously INSANELY jealous of my fabulous new sweater.

And she just couldn't deal with the fact that MY outfit was way CUTER than HER outfit.

Then she pointed at me and snickered. . . .

"UM . . . NIKKI, ARE YOU TRYING TO MAKE
A FASHION STATEMENT? OR HAVE YOU JUST
BEEN EATING OUT OF THE GARBAGE AGAIN?"

That's when I finally looked down at my sweater. Plastered across the front of it was . . .

Brianna's missing sandwich ☹!!

I dropped my diary and just STARED in HORROR!!

No wonder I had gotten so many stares from other students in the hall. But, unfortunately, they hadn't been ADMIRING my new sweater.

That's when I noticed that MacKenzie and practically EVERYONE in the hall were pointing and laughing at me.

Like I was some kind of . . .

FREAK!

Then MacKenzie glared at me and snarled, "Hey, Nikki, would you like some FLIES with that sandwich?! Oops, I mean FRIES!"

And everyone laughed even harder!

I could NOT believe this was actually happening to me.

I just stood there with my mouth dangling wide open.

It was like I was waiting for a SUPERclever comeback to crawl up my throat and jump right into MacKenzie's face.

But I couldn't think of a single thing to say to her.

So I just mumbled, "Whatever."

OMG! I felt SO humiliated!

And embarrassed.

And . . . STUPID!

Blinking back my tears, I picked up my diary and shoved it into my backpack.

Then I slammed my locker door shut and took off running down the hall.

AAAAAAAAAAHH!!!

(That was me screaming in frustration! AGAIN ☹!!)

I've just had the WORST. MORNING. EVER!! And right now I'm hiding out in the girls' bathroom.

I STILL cannot believe that huge FIASCO with MacKenzie! And with Brianna's sandwich!

The only logical explanation is that the sandwich probably got stuck on my coat when I tossed it on the kitchen table this morning.

And then, when I put on my coat, it somehow attached itself to the front of my sweater. Like some kind of, um . . . SUPERfreaky, sticky, slimy . . . ALIEN . . . CREATURE!!

I wanted to rush to the nearest emergency room and BEG the doctors for yet another life-saving medical procedure!! . . .

"DOCTORS, PLEASE HELP ME! CAN YOU
SURGICALLY REMOVE THIS SANDWICH?!"

So Brianna was right. I DID steal her nasty sandwich!

Accidentally ☹!

Anyway, I'm in the bathroom, trying desperately to wipe all the stains off my sweater.

But the situation is hopeless!

I look just like one of Brianna's UGLY finger paintings.

Because now I'm completely covered with:

1. brown peanut-butter stains

2. purple jelly stains

3. white soap suds

AND

4. bright fluorescent-green hand soap from the girls' bathroom.

ME, STARING IN THE MIRROR AND
HAVING A COMPLETE MELTDOWN OVER
THE STAINS ON MY SWEATER!

OMG! It looked like someone had SNARFED down
a cafeteria lunch of tuna casserole, green peas,
blueberry pie, and chocolate milk.

And then THREW UP all over my sweater!!

TWICE ☹!!

I felt absolutely HORRIBLE!

Suddenly, big fat tears started to roll down my
cheeks.

But it wasn't because I was SUPERupset (which
I WAS)!

My eyes were just burning really badly from the
putrid stench of pickle juice. Unfortunately, adding
water to the mix had made the noxious odor ten
times stronger.

That's when I started to cry for real!

My entire school thinks I'm just a huge JOKE!

My favorite sweater (which I had saved up for TWO whole months to buy!!) was TOTALLY RUINED!!!

AND I smelled like a HUMAN PICKLE with very bad body odor!!!

It was ALL Brianna's fault!! Mostly.

Actually, I don't know who makes my life more miserable, MACKENZIE or BRIANNA!

Thank goodness I had my Sassy Sasha perfume with me. I sprayed on practically half the bottle.

So NOW I smell like . . . (*SNIFF SNIFF*) . . .

A PICKLE marinated in Sassy Sasha perfume!!

JUST GREAT ☹!!

Sorry, Brianna! But I'm starting to wish you were NEVER born!

☹!!

In English class, I slouched down in my chair and tried to hide behind my textbook. The last thing I needed was the entire class staring at my hideous stained sweater.

Soon my English teacher came staggering into the class, carrying a massive four-inch-thick book.

She dropped it onto her desk with a loud *THUMP!*

The kids in the front row coughed and fanned the dust cloud it created.

I couldn't help but notice that the ancient book smelled like mildew, fish sticks, and sweaty gym socks.

It smelled as AWFUL as I felt!

Which was a pretty amazing coincidence, when you think about it.

"Good morning, class!" My teacher beamed happily. "Instead of discussing the use of symbolism in our *Grapes of Wrath* novel as originally planned, today we're going to have some fun! So please put away your books."

Everyone happily tossed their *Grapes of Wrath* books on the floor, including me.

Our teacher continued.

"I was cleaning out my attic yesterday and found this awesome treasure!" she exclaimed. "This book of fairy tales belonged to my grandmother and was my favorite book as a child! Fairy tales are an entertaining and fascinating genre in literature."

She picked up the big book and blew the dust off the cover.

Then she proudly held it up for the entire class to see. . . .

MY TEACHER, SHOWING OFF HER
DUSTY OLD BOOK OF FAIRY TALES

"This book actually inspired me to give YOU a
creative writing project today!" she explained.

The entire class groaned, including me.

"Come on, people! This is going to be fun, I promise. Now take out your journals."

I grabbed my English notebook and tried to find a page that wasn't already covered with sketches or doodles.

"I want each of you to rewrite your favorite fairy tale with your own personal twist! It'll be due tomorrow at the end of class. And to get your creative juices flowing, we're going to warm up with a few creative writing exercises.

"A fairy tale is a fictional story that is usually based on folkloric characters such as fairies, goblins, elves, trolls, witches, giants, and talking animals. These stories have their roots in oral traditions, and very similar stories are found in many cultures around the world.

"Every fairy tale has a main character, or protagonist, who is usually a good person. There is often royalty, like a prince, princess, and king and/or queen. Now, for your creative writing exercise,

I want you to fill your journals with ideas for your main character for the next ten minutes. . . ."

Our teacher continued. "Every fairy tale also has an evil character, or antagonist, who tries to harm the good character. This creates the conflict that drives the story. Now fill your page with ideas for your evil character. . . ."

"And finally, there's magic or the granting of a wish. Again, please fill your page with ideas. . . ."

I could have wished that Brianna was never born. But since I'd missed breakfast, I was STARVING! So instead I WISHED I had some FOOD! . . .

"Now let's get started! Try to use some of the ideas from your writing exercises. And feel free to come up and take a look at my book of fairy tales!"

I had to admit, those writing exercises were a lot of fun. I had a ton of great ideas! But I had a really hard time coming up with a story.

I looked around, and the entire room was buzzing with excitement. It seemed everyone was talking about their ideas for their fairy tales.

We were supposed to be brainstorming. But, unfortunately, my brain was farting. I was getting nothing but air.

I've always considered myself a very creative and talented writer. Because, come on, I'm totally addicted to writing in my diary!

But this SUPEReasy, no-rules project was giving me serious anxiety.

That's when I decided to take a look at the fairy tale book to get a few ideas.

My teacher was right! Her book was pretty AWESOME. . . .

ME, TOTALLY LOST IN THE
FASCINATING FAIRY TALE WORLD!

By the end of the hour, everyone was busy writing . . . except ME ☹!

Instead, I had spent the entire class completely absorbed in an exciting fairy tale adventure.

Reading about tearjerking love stories and thrilling adventures was a great escape from my OWN very MUNDANE and extremely CRUDDY existence.

But I still didn't have the slightest idea what I was going to write. I left class more frustrated and discouraged than ever.

I trudged off to my French class, hugging my books, trying to hide the nasty stain on my sweater.

But kids still pointed at me and snickered.

Right now I feel HORRIBLE! Sometimes I wish I could wave a magic wand and disappear!

After my French and social studies classes were finally over, I went back to my locker to wait for my BFFs, Chloe and Zoey.

We meet there every day to walk together to gym class. I was surprised when Brandon rushed up to me.

"Hi, Nikki! I've been looking for you all morning. I hope you got my texts! And, um . . . WOW! What happened to your sweater?!"

"What's up, Brandon? I just had a little accident. With a sandwich. But I'm fine. So, you sent me a text?"

"Yeah. Actually, I sent you three. They were pretty important! The journalism camp I'm going to this summer has an opening for a cartoonist. I guess someone from another school canceled."

"Really? That sounds, um . . . interesting," I said, trying to be coolly nonchalant.

BRANDON AND ME, DISCUSSING GOING TO
SUMMER CAMP TOGETHER ☺!!

But in the deepest depths of my inner soul, I was
literally screaming . . .

OMG! OMG! I COULD JUST DIE AT THE THOUGHT
OF POSSIBLY SPENDING THE ENTIRE SUMMER
HANGING OUT AT CAMP WITH BRANDON,

TAKING LONG, ROMANTIC WALKS THROUGH THE WOODS HAND IN HAND, BREATHLESSLY GAZING INTO EACH OTHER'S EYES WHILE BEING EATEN ALIVE BY MOSQUITOES!! SQUEEEEEE ☺!!

"Nikki, Mr. Zimmerman said he wants to add a comic strip to our school newspaper. And he's willing to pay for either you or MacKenzie to go to camp, since you're both talented artists. Anyway, I was hoping it was YOU who signed up, because it looks like the spot has already been—"

"Hold on, Brandon. Let me check my phone. Now that I think about it, I haven't gotten ANYTHING from ANYONE all morning, which is VERY strange."

That's when I took out my cell phone to check my calls and messages. And Brandon suddenly got this really puzzled look on his face.

"So, where did you get your phone case? It's definitely very, um . . . different!" he asked.

"Actually, I got it last month at the mall."

BRANDON, WONDERING WHAT'S UP
WITH MY PHONE!

However, when I tried to retrieve the text messages Brandon had sent me, I had two small problems. . . .

First, my cell phone battery was completely DEAD! Which meant Brianna was playing the Princess Sugar Plum games on it without my permission. AGAIN! ☹!!

Second, my eyes were about to rupture and BLEED from the terribly tacky self-portrait she had drawn on my PHONE with a black marker ☹!!!

↑ BRIANNA'S SELF-PORTRAIT

ME, IN SHOCK AT WHAT BRIANNA HAD DONE TO MY POOR PHONE!!

But the most disappointing thing was that because I never got Brandon's text messages, MacKenzie will probably be the one spending the summer at camp with Brandon, being eaten alive by mosquitoes, not ME ☹!!

I was CRUSHED! And Brandon was pretty bummed about it too.

Although I felt like crying (AGAIN!), I plastered a big smile across my face and told him how much I appreciated him texting me the camp information, even though I never got a chance to read it because my phone battery was dead.

He kind of shrugged and stuck his hands in his pockets. "Hey, no problem. I guess there's always next year. Right? Anyway, I'll see you in bio."

"Sure. And thanks again," I said as he headed down the hall.

I sighed in frustration and then collapsed against my locker.

It looks like my day is getting CRUDDIER and CRUDDIER by the hour.

Seriously!

I don't know how much more of this DRAMA I can take!!

☹!!

Good news! I've FINALLY come up with a brilliant plan for how to fix my stained sweater situation.

After gym, I plan to go to the office and call my mom to come pick me up and take me home.

Then I'll take a quick shower so I won't smell like Sassy Sasha and pickle juice.

And after I've changed my clothes, I plan to bury my sweater in the backyard!

If I hurry, I might actually make it back to school in time for bio and get to see Brandon again ☺!

One thing is for sure, I don't know how I would make it at this school without my BFFs, Chloe and Zoey!

No matter how bad I'm feeling, they always manage to make me laugh and lift my spirits. And today was no different.

I told them about all the drama with Brianna, MacKenzie, and Brandon. And then I showed them my messed-up sweater and the graffiti on my phone case. They just stared at me in horror. . . .

ME, SHOWING MY HORRIFIED BFFS
MY MESSED-UP SWEATER
AND THE GRAFFITI ON MY PHONE!

Chloe said, "OMG, Nikki! You poor thing! I feel SO sorry for you!"

And Zoey said, "'When things are bad, we take a bit of comfort in the thought that they could always be WORSE. And when they are, we find hope in the thought that things are so bad they have to get BETTER.'—Malcolm S. Forbes."

Then they both gave me a BIG hug!

So right now I'm feeling a lot better.

Chloe and Zoey are the BEST friends EVER!!!

☺!!

I could hardly wait for gym to be over so I could finally go home and change.

As we were finishing up our warm-up exercises, our teacher disappeared into the storage closet.

That meant only one thing! We were going to be doing some type of activity with a ball!

JUST GREAT ☹!

She was going to emerge with a basketball, soccer ball, volleyball, baseball, or maybe a football.

Sorry, but I was starving! The only ball I wanted to get up close and personal with right then was a juicy meatball or a savory cheese ball. YUM!!

Unfortunately, my food fantasy was rudely interrupted when the teacher blew her whistle and announced the most HATED gym class activity known to humankind. . . .

Then our teacher threw the balls out on the gym floor and the game began. All the athletic kids immediately scrambled for a ball.

Being the first person out is the ultimate humiliation.

Everyone jeers and makes the L for "loser" sign with their fingers while you slowly do your "walk of shame" to the bleachers.

I wasn't about to let that happen to me!

AGAIN!!

But just in case it DID, I had tucked my diary and pen inside my shirt so I could make good use of my downtime on the bleachers.

I immediately noticed Jessica staring at me the way a hungry snake stares at a mouse. And YIKES! Unfortunately for me, she had a ball in her hands.

Suddenly she took off running toward me.

I bobbed and weaved through the cross fire of flying balls like a pro until she somehow trapped me in a corner.

"Ha! There's nowhere to run now!" She grinned. "Eat rubber, DORK!"

She threw the ball at me, but I ducked just in the nick of time. As the ball ricocheted off the wall, her eyes got as large as saucers.

"UH-OH!" she whimpered, and quickly turned to try to run away.

But the ball smacked her right on her butt!

WHOP!!

"You're OUT! You're OUT!" a boy cried gleefully as he pointed at her.

"YES!!" I shouted in triumph as I did my Snoopy "happy dance" right there on the gym floor.

Jessica was the FIRST person out of the game!!

While the other kids taunted Jessica, I leaned against the wall to catch my breath. Chloe and Zoey excitedly ran up to me and gave me high fives.

"OMG!" Chloe cried. "I thought Jessica had you for sure!"

"Nikki, just take deep breaths," Zoey huffed. "You sound like you're hyperventilating!"

"I'm f-f-fine!" I panted. "But that was close! I thought I was DEAD!"

We'd only been standing there for a few seconds. Then, before I could even scream "WATCH OUT!!" a group of jocks started whipping balls at us like we were giant teddy bears in a carnival arcade game or something.

OMG! We could feel the rush of cool air as the balls whizzed by, just missing our heads.

Chloe, Zoey, and I just FROZE like deer in headlights. . . .

ME AND MY BFFS, GETTING AMBUSHED!

"Well, girlfriends! It's the three of us against the world! And, personally, I think we're DOOMED!" Chloe groaned.

"Come on, guys! Don't give up yet!" Zoey said. "If we're moving targets, they'll have a harder time hitting us. SCATTER! And whatever you do, DON'T. STOP. RUNNING!"

So we took off in different directions, running around the gym like headless chickens.

We ran in circles, zigzags, and swirls. And that strategy really seemed to work.

Because somehow my BFFs and I managed to survive the game. Soon it was down to just the three of us and a few others.

This was the longest we had EVER lasted!

That's when we started to really get into the game. We were running, catching, throwing, and dodging like Olympians. It was actually a lot of fun! . . . .

ME AND MY BFFS, HAVING A BLAST
PLAYING DODGEBALL ☺!!

Until MacKenzie suddenly appeared out of nowhere and screamed . . .

"HEY, MAXWELL! EAT THIS!"

She threw the ball at me as hard as she could! . . . .

And then . . .

WHAM!

OMG!

I got hit right in the face!!!

It felt like that ball was going one hundred miles an hour.

Suddenly everything was hazy and in slow motion.

I tried to walk to the bleachers, but my legs felt all squishy, like jelly.

Something was wrong.

VERY wrong!

My BFFs' voices sounded really, really far away, almost like an echo.

"Nikkiiiiiiiiiiii!" Zoey cried. "Someone get the teacherrrrr!"

"Oh noooooo!" Chloe screamed. "I think she's huuuurt! Helllllp!"

My head was spinning like crazy!

And so was the room!

That's when I lost my balance and felt myself falling.

Then everything went pitch-black.

☹!!

DESCENDING INTO THE DEEPEST
DEPTHS OF DARKNESS

When I finally opened my eyes, I was surrounded by darkness.

I was completely disoriented and had the weirdest sensation of intense butterflies in my stomach.
It was the same exact feeling you get on a roller coaster.

It actually felt like I was . . . falling?!

YES! That was it!!

OH, CRUD!!!

I was FALLING!!!

And falling . . .

And falling . . .

And FALLING ☹!! . . .

SOMEPLACE REALLY WEIRD!!

The only thing I knew for sure was that I WASN'T sure about ANYTHING anymore.

I wasn't sure if I was actually AWAKE and just THOUGHT I was DREAMING! Or if I was actually DREAMING and just THOUGHT I was AWAKE!

I wasn't sure what was reality and what was fantasy.

I was asleep (I think) when suddenly I heard voices.

"Everyone stand back! Give her room to breathe!" said a guy whose voice I didn't recognize.

"Do you think she's still alive?" asked a girl.

"I'm not sure. She looks kind of dead to me. See how dull and lifeless her skin is?" another guy replied.

I was like, Sorry, dude! Unlike MacKenzie, I DON'T have a lifetime membership to You-Pay-We-Spray! tanning salon.

NOTE TO SELF: ALWAYS use blush and bronzing powder. Because you never know when you'll wake up surrounded by a group of insensitive beauty critics who mistake you for DEAD!

"Very good point," another girl agreed. "She looks DEAD to me, too!"

"Oh well! She's lucky the fall killed her BEFORE the Wicked Witch of the West did!" said the second guy.

"Hey, let's check her pockets for munchies!" suggested a third guy.

"Good idea!" the first guy exclaimed. "After all, dead people don't eat snacks. Usually."

Okay, this conversation was, like, way TOO weird!

That's when I suddenly opened my eyes. I was completely surrounded by a group of blurry faces staring at me. . . .

A GROUP OF VERY STRANGE KIDS,
STARING AT ME AND MISTAKING ME
FOR DEAD!

"Not so fast!" I shouted. "I'm NOT dead! YET!"

The startled group gasped and cautiously backed away from me.

Then they quietly whispered among themselves, "She's NOT dead?! Nope! Not dead at all!"

I slowly sat up and looked around. I was on the floor in the gym.

But I had no idea who those kids were.

They were shorter than me, oddly dressed, and covered in . . . what looked like, um . . .

JUNK FOOD?!!

They had candy and popcorn stuck in their hair, chocolate and peanut butter smears on their clothing, and sticky hands and faces.

Those kids' clothing was covered in more food stains than my new sweater. . . .

It was like I had single-handedly started a "sloppy chic" fashion craze.

"Well, dip my chip! She's ALIVE after all!" the first guy exclaimed as he gave me a warm smile. "This is awkward! Please accept our sincerest apologies."

"No problem," I muttered as I staggered to my feet, still slightly dizzy. "Ugh! I don't feel so good!"

"I know what will make you feel better!" a small girl said shyly. "How about a lollipop?"

Actually, that sounded like a great idea. I hadn't eaten all day, and I was starving.

The little girl pulled a sucker out of her dark curly hair and offered it to me.

At first glance, it looked like the candy was coated with powdered sugar. YUM!!

But upon closer inspection, I realized it was lint and dandruff!

With a few stray hairs!

EWW ☹!!

I plastered a big smile across my face to keep from gagging. . . .

MUNCHKIN GIRL, OFFERING ME
A HAIRY, LINTY, DANDRUFF-COVERED
LOLLIPOP!

"Gee, thanks, hon! But I just had lunch," I lied.

Then the entire group crowded around and
stared at me as they munched loudly on their
snacks. . . .

VERY STRANGE KIDS, STARING AT ME AS

THEY MUNCH ON SNACKS

"I'm Chip. Nice to meet you!" the first guy finally said, and extended his hand. It was greasy and covered with crumbled potato chips, but I shook it anyway.

"Hi, I'm Nikki! I'm glad to meet you and all of, um . . . your friends."

"It's a miracle you actually survived that ordeal!" Chip said, with a mouthful of chips.

I quickly glanced around the gym and realized I didn't see ANYONE from my P.E. class.

"Is my class already over? I've never seen any of you before. You must be sixth graders," I said.

What was going on?!

I vaguely remembered MacKenzie SLAMMING me in the face with a ball during a game of dodgeball. And me feeling faint and falling.

Chloe and Zoey had totally panicked and screamed for help and—

Wait a minute!! WHERE were Chloe and Zoey?!!

Had they just left me lying there on the floor and rushed off to their next class?!

Clearly, none of these people were in MY gym class. Heck, I didn't even recognize them as attending my SCHOOL!!

I suddenly felt woozy due to another dizzy spell. Where was the ding-dang school nurse when you really needed her?

And, more important, where was my gym teacher?

Maybe she could explain what was going on. And give me a pass, since I was obviously late for lunch and possibly even bio.

As I slowly limped toward the gym door to leave, it felt like my entire face had been rearranged.

I probably had two black eyes, a busted lip, a chipped tooth, AND a broken nose ☹!!

407

I was going straight to the office to call my parents to go HOME.

"Good-bye! And thank you for taking care of that evil witch for us! You're our HERO!" Chip cheered as the other students joined in.

I stopped in my tracks and slowly turned around.

"Um, WHAT evil witch? And HOW exactly did I take care of her?" I asked, trying desperately to remember what had happened. "And, um . . . WHO are you guys?"

"Well, we're Munchkins, and we attend Fairy Tale Land Middle School along with all the other storybook characters. MacKenzie, the Wicked Witch of the West, always stole our munchies," Chip explained. "Until YOU came along!"

"MUNCHKINS?! You're kidding me!" I said, glancing around the room for hidden cameras. "Okay! I'm being PUNKED by Chloe and Zoey for some TV show or something! Right?!"

"It's very possible. But I don't know any Munchkins named Chloe or Zoey. Are they Regals, Renegades, or Rogues?"

"HUH?!" I blinked in confusion. "I don't have any idea what you're talking—"

"You know! The stuff we learned in Introduction to Storybook Family Genealogy," Chip said.

"Regals are royalty, like kings, queens, princes, and princesses," said Lollipop Girl.

"Renegades are the brave adventurers who hang out in the woods," said a guy munching on a slice of pizza.

"And the Rogues are magic users, like the witch!" said a girl with a mouthful of cotton candy.

"And the fairies, too! They're the caretakers of Fairy Tale Land!" explained Chip. "Us Munchkins are Renegades."

"You guys CAN'T be serious!" I laughed nervously.

"We're VERY serious. As a heart attack. Totally!" the group answered solemnly.

My laughter grew a little more shrill and jittery.

For some reason this whole story sounded vaguely familiar.

Then it hit me!

OMG! Maybe I was in the story of *The Wonderful Wizard of Oz!*

Only THESE Munchkins actually munched munchies?!!

Or it was very possible that I'd gone completely INSANE!

"No way!" I gasped as my laughter turned into a frantic sob. "This CAN'T be real! OMG! I got hit in the face with a ball by MacKenzie, and now I'm suffering from BRAIN DAMAGE!!" I shrieked hysterically.

Lollipop Girl gave me a big hug.

"Don't worry! That mean witch won't bother you anymore. You really gave her a licking!" She giggled.

"Yeah!" Chip chimed in. "You whipped her butt like mashed potatoes!"

"You totally creamed her!" said a boy with a drippy ice-cream cone. "Just like this . . . !"

He demonstrated by greedily gobbling the entire thing in one bite, and then belched loudly.

I gaped in horror, imagining his scoop of Chunky Monkey ice cream as MacKenzie's head.

Sure, I sort of hated that girl a little bit. But I'd NEVER go cannibal and bite her head off!

Although I was pretty sure her head was completely hollow.

Just saying!

"What exactly did I do to her?" I asked nervously. "I don't remember a thing!"

"Well, the witch was standing right here, bullying us and stealing our snacks. Until you fell out of the sky and CLOBBERED her!" said Pizza Boy.

Okay, I DID kind of remember the falling part.

But nothing about a WITCH.

"You were AWESOME!!" Chip gushed. "You landed right on top of her! We actually took pictures. Wanna see them?"

"Um, SURE!" I answered.

He pulled some photos out of his jacket pocket.

"Here's a pic of the witch bullying us. Those wedgies were pretty brutal. . . ."

THE WICKED WITCH OF THE WEST,
BULLYING MUNCHKINS INTO GIVING UP
THEIR MUNCHIES!!

I couldn't believe my eyes!

MacKenzie was dressed in a very fashionable witch
outfit and torturing two Munchkins with double
wedgies! OUCH ☹!!

Chip continued. "And here you are, valiantly coming to our rescue!" . . .

ME, FALLING OUT OF THE SKY,
ABOUT TO CLOBBER
THE WICKED WITCH OF THE WEST

"And then . . . POW!!" Chip shouted excitedly. "You took her out and saved us Munchkins!!" . . .

ME, CLOBBERING THE WITCH!

OMG! It was true! I'd actually landed on the Wicked Witch of the West!!!

I would not have believed that ANY of this had happened if I had not seen the photos with my very own eyes.

"And the final pic is of me and my friends getting even with the witch," Chip explained. "As you can see, I'm really good at drawing mustaches!" . . .

THE MUNCHKINS, DRAWING A MUSTACHE
AND ASSORTED GRAFFITI ON THE FACE
OF THE WICKED WITCH OF THE WEST

OMG! That photo of her just lying there pushed me over the edge, and I TOTALLY lost it!!

"OH NO! I've KILLED MacKenzie!" I wailed. "It was totally an accident. OMG! She's . . . DEAD!! Where's her b-body?!"

"Probably in the school nurse's office," Chip answered. "She woke up right before you did. She's NOT dead. Just REALLY ticked off!"

"Thank goodness! At least I didn't kill her!" I muttered, feeling relieved.

I was NOT a murderer! Woo-hoo ☺!

"Nope! You just ripped her skinny jeans, smeared her lip gloss, broke three fingernails, tore out five hair extensions, and knocked her out of her designer shoes!" giggled Lollipop Girl.

For MacKenzie, suffering all of that public humiliation was probably WORSE than murder!!

That's when I noticed the cutest pair of platform sneakers lying right in the middle of the gym floor. . . .

417

THE WICKED WITCH OF THE WEST'S
SUPERCUTE DESIGNER SHOES!

I had to admit, those platform sneakers were to
DIE for!

"Anyway, the witch was really angry. She said she

was going to hop on her broom and zoom off to the salon for an emergency appointment to get her hair and nails done, right after she visited the school nurse," Chip explained.

"You probably would have been better off accidentally killing her. Because now she's probably going to try and kill YOU!!" a girl with a cupcake said sadly as she wiped away a tear.

"Kill you dead! So sad!" the Munchkins murmured solemnly among themselves.

"Just great! The last thing I need right now is a wicked witch hunting me down. I just want to go HOME!" I whined.

"Well, you could always ask the Good Witch of the North to help you!" Lollipop Girl said. "She's nice, friendly, and powerful."

"I'm going to need all the help I can get. The Wicked Witch of the West sounds like a real drama queen," I said, starting to worry.

Suddenly there was a flash of light, and everyone pointed toward the ceiling. . . .

"Look! There she is right now!" Chip exclaimed.

"WHO? The Wicked Witch . . . ?!" I gulped.

She was the LAST person I wanted to see!

It was DEFINITELY time for me to leave.

Where is a TORNADO when you really need one?

☹!!

WHICH WITCH IS WHICH?!

I stared in amazement as colorful sprinkles rained down around the room and then disappeared into the air.

I gasped when a little girl appeared, wearing a pink Princess Sugar Plum costume and a HUGE crown. She was carrying a wand that was almost taller than she was.

"BRIANNA?!" I shrieked excitedly. "OMG! I'm SO happy to see you! What are you doing in my gym class? Do Mom and Dad know you're here?"

"Hey, slow your roll, sister," Brianna said, glaring at me. "I don't think we've met before!"

"Of course we've MET! You're my SISTER! Don't you recognize me? You just called me your sister a second ago!"

"Actually, THAT was sarcasm!" Brianna said, rather, um . . . sarcastically.

"Well, you LOOK just like my little sister!" I said, folding my arms and eyeing her suspiciously.

"Sorry, but I'm NOT! I'm Brianna the Fairy Godmother, at your service!" she said, and curtsied. "I also work part-time as the Good Witch of the North on Tuesdays and Thursdays." She handed me a business card written sloppily in crayon. It said . . .

WISHES & ENCHANTMENTS BY BRIANNA

You dream, I deliver—Since 1583

Brianna the Fairy Godmother

a.k.a. Good Witch of the North

President & CEO

(555) 555-0111

Then she gave me a big, warm smile. . . .

BRIANNA, THE FAIRY GODMOTHER
AND THE GOOD WITCH OF THE NORTH!!

423

"Wow! You've been in business for a long time!"
I exclaimed.

"That's right. I've got centuries' worth of experience.
And I look really good for my age too, don't I?" she
said, admiring her reflection in her wand. "Anyway,
let's talk about YOU! My new client!" She pushed
several buttons on the base of her wand.

Suddenly the star dinged and lit up, just like a
smartphone.

She read her wand and then stared at me as she
tapped her chin in thought.

"Hmm. This says you've traveled to our world from
an alternate universe. And it looks to me like you
were knocked unconscious at some point," Brianna
announced matter-of-factly.

"Wow! How did you know that?!" I asked, amazed.

"Simple. My smartwand calculated where you're from.
The other part was just my lucky guess. OMG! What

424

happened? It looks like you got hit in the face with a shovel! OUCH!"

That's when I just glared at that girl in complete disgust.

I could NOT believe she was actually talking about my face like that right to my . . . um, FACE.

There was an awkward silence.

Then Brianna giggled nervously. "So, Nikki, what can I help you with today? Anything you want, just ask! However, I must warn you that temporary makeovers only come with a twelve-hour warranty."

"Well, right now I just want to go home! I'm supposed to babysit my sister later today. And I have a really bad feeling I'm going to have a very angry wicked witch hunting me down very soon."

Brianna giggled. "Yeah! You fell right out of the sky, and BAM!! It was HILARIOUS! I saw the video on WhoTube. It's already gone viral!"

"Wait, don't you mean YouTube?" I asked.

"No, it's WHOTUBE!"

"But the correct name is YOUTUBE."

"No! It's WhoTube, Miss Smarty-Pants!" Brianna said, rolling her eyes at me.

"Whatever!" I answered.

"Now, pay close attention! The BEST way to get home is to go to the office. Once there, you're going to ask for an appointment to see the Great and Powerful Wizard of—"

"OZ!" I interrupted. "It's Oz, right? I already know the story!"

"WRONG!" Brianna snapped. "It's the Great and Powerful Wizard of ODD!"

"ODD?! Don't you mean OZ?" I asked.

"No! It's ODD! And please DON'T interrupt me again! If anyone has the power to get you home, it's the Wizard of Odd, also known as Principal Winston. He's got a thick pad of PASSES that can magically transport you anywhere with the mere stroke of his pen. But be careful, because there are also detentions and suspensions lurking around that place. Got it?"

"Got it!" I answered eagerly.

"Also, I'm going to give you this pair of shoes. They have the power to—"

"I know the story!" I interrupted. "Transport me HOME! Right?!"

"WRONG!! They have the power to magically style you from head to toe in one cute outfit!" Brianna explained.

"Oh! Is that all those shoes will do?" I asked, a little disappointed. "I was hoping for a pair of those glittery magic slippers like Dorothy's."

"The Wicked Witch of the West is very vain. HER shoes don't transport. They just STYLE. Sorry!" Brianna said.

Then she dramatically pointed her wand at the platform sneakers.

"Please, everyone needs to stand back at least twelve feet from my wand. It's just a safety precaution to limit your exposure to random magic particles."

Everyone in the room scooted back a bit, and Brianna began a magic chant. . . .

> "Platform sneakers,
> fashionably sweet!
> Find your new home
> on Nikki's, um . . .
> STREET!"

Then she dramatically waved her magic wand, and . . .

Absolutely NOTHING happened! ☹!!

I sighed and tried not to roll my eyes.

Gravely concerned about this recent turn of events, all the Munchkins spoke in hushed tones among themselves.

Brianna, obviously embarrassed, impatiently smacked her wand on the palm of her hand a few times.

"Come ON! I just put new batteries in this thing yesterday!" she muttered.

I didn't want to seem obnoxious or anything, but my guess was that her magic spell was a little off.

"Um, do you think maybe you should have said 'FEET,' instead of 'STREET'? It's just a suggestion. You're totally the expert on magic here!" I said, shrugging my shoulders.

Brianna wrinkled up her nose at me. "I already thought of THAT, Miss Smarty-Pants! So don't tell me how to do my job." She cleared her throat rather loudly and tried the magic chant again. . . .

> "Platform sneakers,
> fashionably sweet!
> Find your new home
> on Nikki's . . .
> FEET!"

Brianna waved her wand, and this time the shoes magically appeared on my feet.

"They belonged to the Wicked Witch of the West, but now they're all yours!" Brianna beamed proudly.

"Thanks! But won't she be a little irritated that I'm wearing her shoes?" I asked.

"Actually, she's going to be FURIOUS! But let's face it. You need them a lot more than she does!" Brianna said matter-of-factly.

"Well, if the shoes won't help me get home, WHY do I even need them?" I grumbled.

"Because your old sneakers STANK! When was the last time you washed those things? They smelled like sardines and baby burp!" Brianna said, fanning her nose.

Even though I was highly insulted, I had to admit Brianna had a really good point.

My mom was forever complaining about exactly the same thing.

Even though I wore them daily in gym class, it had probably been a year since I had washed those sneakers.

I've been needing a new pair of shoes for gym for quite a while now.

Anyway, the new shoes were a PERFECT fit.

And they looked even cuter on. . . .

ME, ADMIRING MY NEW SHOES! (WELL,
ACTUALLY, THE WITCH'S SHOES)

I thanked my fairy godmother for her help and then said good-bye to all my new Munchkin friends. Then I kind of stood there, waiting patiently for Brianna to use her magic wand thingy again.

"Okay, so what's the problem NOW?" she huffed.

"Um . . . aren't you supposed to help me magically find the Wizard of Odd? You know, like in the story."

"NO! But it looks like YOU'RE trying to tell ME how to do my job again!" Brianna snarked.

"Of course not! I—I was just wondering how I'm ever going to find the wizard if I don't have a yellow brick road to follow. Or maybe you can whip up one of those GPS thingies."

Brianna rolled her eyes.

"Simple! His office is where it's ALWAYS been. Just go out this door and down the hall. It's the first door on the right!"

"Um . . . okay. Thanks!" I mumbled, feeling kind of stupid.

Then I turned and rushed toward the gym door.

I planned to go straight to the Fairy Tale Land Middle School office and find the Wizard of Odd. He'd give me a pass to go home, and then I'd call my mom to pick me up. She'd take one look at my sad, puppy-dog eyes, and soon I'd be snuggled in my comfy bed, eating a pint of Ben & Jerry's ice cream with an ice pack on my face.

Yep! I was starting to feel better already.

My day had been one never-ending horror story. But soon my very weird adventure in Fairy Tale Land was going to have a HAPPY ENDING!

!!

OMG! I'm totally FREAKING out right now! Things around here are getting more bizarre by the minute!

I exited the gym door just like my fairy godmother, Brianna, had instructed. But there wasn't a hallway outside that door!

NOPE! Just a DARK, CREEPY FOREST!!! ☹!!! And, unfortunately, I'm very ALLERGIC to dark, creepy forests!

I gasped and blinked a few times just to make sure my eyes weren't playing tricks on me.

Then, in a panic, I turned around and tried to rush back to the safety of the gym. But THAT was no longer an option. The door had disappeared into thin air! ☹!!

With the full moon, the huge trees cast spooky shadows that made it even more difficult to see in the darkness.

436

I felt like I was in one of those scary slasher movies that my parents won't let me watch. However, on a more positive note, my enchanted shoes worked like a charm ☺!

They magically changed my drab gym clothes into a SUPERcute sky-blue dress with a white apron, tights, and shiny black Mary Jane shoes.

Which, for some reason, looked vaguely familiar. . . .

Then it occurred to me that I was dressed just like my favorite storybook character, Alice from *Alice's Adventures in Wonderland!* SQUEEEE ☺!!!

But I digress. . . .

Suddenly I had the very creepy sensation that someone was watching me. As the wind started to howl, I spotted a pair of sinister glowing red eyes staring right at me ☹!!

That's when I screamed and started running through the woods as fast as I could. . . .

438

I wandered through the forest, totally lost, for what seemed like . . .

FOREVER!

Then cold, hungry, and frightened, I collapsed in exhaustion in front of a huge rock.

How was I ever going to get out of this place?!

That's when I suddenly remembered that I had a fairy godmother.

THANK GOODNESS ☺!!

I cleared my throat and whispered loudly, "Um . . . Brianna! Can you help me? PLEASE!"

But there was no response.

So I tried yelling as loud as I could. . . .

"BRIANNA!!! HELP!!"

But the only response I got was a very peculiar echo: "BRIANNA HELP! BRIANNA HELP! BRIANNA HELP!"

It quickly became very apparent to me that I was in this calamity all alone.

NOTE TO SELF:
Find a NEW fairy godmother!!

I took three deep breaths and tried to calm myself.

The last thing I needed to do right then was have a complete meltdown.

Especially since I'd already had three or four today.

I finally came to the logical conclusion that it would probably be easier to find my way out of the forest in the morning.

Assuming, of course, I SURVIVED the night ☹!

ME, LOST AND ALONE
IN THE DARK, CREEPY FOREST!!

So I just sat there next to that big rock, staring
into the darkness, hugging my knees and rocking

back and forth, wishing I was back home with my OWN family, in my OWN room, snuggled in my OWN comfy bed.

And hoping those scary red eyes staring back at me didn't belong to a ferocious animal with really sharp teeth that ATE kids who got slammed in the face during gym, woke up in another world, and ended up lost in the woods in the middle of the night.

Then I finally fell into a deep, fretful sleep.

☹!!

FURRY AND FEATHERED FRIENDS!

I awoke the next morning to the warmth of the sun on my face and the happy sounds of birds chirping.

At first I was dazed and confused.

Why did my pillow feel as hard as a rock? And how did an assortment of furry and feathered critters get into my bedroom?!

That's when all the memories came flooding back into my mind like a tidal wave. I was stuck in some strange storybook land and needed to get back home!

I stretched, got to my feet, and looked around.

The forest looked nothing WHATSOEVER like I remembered from last night.

I couldn't help but smile. I felt just like a Disney princess or something. . . .

ME, WITH MY NEW WOODLAND
CREATURE FRIENDS!

OMG! All those adorable little animals were really friendly. I felt like dancing and singing with them, just like in those sappy movies.

And get this! They even brought me an assortment of fruits, nuts, and berries for breakfast. Which made me VERY happy because I was literally STARVING!!

Yesterday I missed breakfast, lunch, AND dinner. OMG! I was SO hungry I could have chewed the bark right off of a tree!

I ate the delicious treats and stuffed the leftovers in my pockets.

Next, I happily thanked all my newfound friends for their generosity.

No longer exhausted or hungry, I set out to find my way back home.

INTO THE WOODS

One thing was for sure—I definitely liked the friendly, happy daytime woods a lot better than the dark, creepy nighttime woods.

Somehow, I had to find the Wizard of Odd. But I doubted that his office was in the middle of the woods.

I tried not to think about the "what-ifs."

What if I didn't find the wizard?

What if I couldn't find my way back home?

What if I was stuck in this place . . . FOREVER?

About ten minutes into my journey, I stumbled upon a well-worn, winding path and decided to follow it.

I hadn't traveled more than a half mile when I made the most AMAZING discovery. . . .

It was the cutest little cottage I had ever seen!

And it was obviously inhabited, because of the manicured lawn and flowers. I was sure the people living there could help me!

They probably knew the Wizard of Odd. Or knew someone who knew the Wizard of Odd. Or knew someone who knew someone who knew the Wizard of Odd.

HOPEFULLY!

And if they had a phone, I could call my mom and tell her not to worry because I'd be home soon.

I felt really happy and relieved that this whole FIASCO was going to be over.

I excitedly ran to the door and knocked. But no one answered. I knocked again even harder, but still no answer. Then I pounded kind of desperately.

That's when, to my surprise, the door slowly swung open. I poked my head inside.

"Hello? Is anyone home?" I called out.

Since it was kind of an emergency, I stepped inside to have a look around. . . .

SOMEONE HAD EATEN THE SMALLEST BOWL OF PORRIDGE. . . .

SOMEONE HAD SAT IN AND BROKEN THE
SMALLEST CHAIR. . . .

AND THAT SOMEONE WAS STILL SLEEPING IN
THE SMALLEST BED!!

It was a young girl about my age with beautiful curly blond hair. But when I leaned over and took a closer look at her face, I totally freaked out.

"CHLOE?!! OMG! CHLOE!!" I screamed, shaking her awake. "It's me, Nikki! I'm SO happy to see you!"

Startled, the poor girl opened her eyes and sat straight up in the bed, staring at me like I was a lunatic.

"Chloe, it's ME! Nikki! How did YOU get here?" I shouted. "And when did you change your hair?! It's really cute!"

"Actually, my name isn't Chloe. It's Goldilocks! And I don't believe we've ever met before," the girl said as she looked me up and down.

Then a smile slowly spread across her face. "Wait a minute! I DO recognize you! Blue dress and white apron—you're Dorothy from *The Wonderful Wizard of Oz*, right?! You sat in front of me in Managing Dangerous Fairy Tale Animals: Lions, Tigers, and Bears class, right?!"

"Actually, no! I'm sorry, but—"

"No? Are you sure?" Goldilocks said, squinting at me. "Hmm. Now I remember! We were in the same study group for Surviving the Dark, Dangerous Forest: Tips and Tactics! And wasn't Professor Huntsman HAWT? I wouldn't mind flunking that final exam just to be in HIS class again," she gushed. "Right, Dorothy?"

"Sorry, but I'M NOT DOROTHY!!" I said.

Goldilocks stared at me and tapped her chin in thought.

Finally, she smiled again.

"Of course NOT! Everyone was always mixing up you and Dorothy. You're Alice from *Alice's Adventures in Wonderland*, right? Blue dress, white apron! You and Dorothy are practically twins. I think you and I both had the class Eating on a Budget in Fairy Tale Land: Why Pay When You Can Beg, Borrow, and Steal, and Eat for FREE?"

"Um . . . actually, I'm NOT—"

"And how could I forget!" Goldilocks interrupted.
"For your class project, you swallowed 'Drink Me!'
juice from that little bottle. Then you grew to
ten feet and then shrank to ten inches. It was
AWESOME! You totally deserved that A-plus, Alice!"

GOLDILOCKS, RAMBLING ON AND ON ABOUT
STUFF AND CALLING ME ALICE ☹!!

Okay, now I was starting to get a little frustrated. **I wasn't Dorothy OR Alice!**

"Well, my outfit is kind of a complicated story. I might be dressed like Alice, but I'm really—"

"You know what, Alice, I think you should petition the Fairy Tale Land Council to change your dress color. Now, yellow is way too bright. And green is way too dark! But PINK! That would be JUST right! And then people wouldn't always confuse you with Dorothy. So, do you like porridge? There are two bowls left on the table. I think I'm getting hungry again. . . ."

OMG!! Goldilocks was REEEALLY talkative!!

"To be honest, Goldilocks, I don't think that's such a good idea. What if the bears are hungry too? They might be a little upset when they come home and find all of their porridge gone," I said, starting to worry about that very issue myself.

"Bears?! Did you just say 'BEARS'?!" Goldilocks gasped, looking very alarmed.

"Yes, I did! The Three Bears live in this house!" I explained. "And if I remember the story correctly, they'll be arriving here any minute now."

"Are you sure BEARS live here? I was told by one of the Rogues that this place was a brand-new bed-and-breakfast and I could just drop in anytime since no reservations were required. But now it's starting to make sense. The service is bad, the food is bland, the furniture is cheap, the support staff is nonexistent, and my bed is a little lumpy. As a hotel this place STINKS! Next time, I'm staying at the Fairyott Hotel."

Goldilocks COMPLAINED an awful lot too.

"A Rogue? That's a magic user, right?" I said.

"It was the Wicked Witch of the West, actually. Her name is MacKenzie and she's in my Survey of Fairy Tale Land History class. Rumpelstiltskin is the most BORING history teacher EVER! Sleeping Beauty pretty much snoozes through ALL of his classes. Although, to be honest, that girl snoozes through EVERYTHING!"

"Wow, it sounds like a really fascinating class!" I said.

"Well, it's NOT! After the Great War, Fairy Tale Land was divided into three groups. The REGALS are all of the royalty. They're the lucky ones with perfect lives! And they always get a happily ever after. They have SUPERactive social lives with lots of parties, balls, and weddings. Hey, I'd love to have gourmet food, servants, and a closet full of gorgeous silk dresses and be pampered all day. Most of them are a little spoiled, if you ask me!"

"Yeah, it does sound like they have a lot of fun! I can see why you feel that way," I said.

"The RENEGADES are adventurers. They're courageous and try to help others. That's what I am. But I'm BORED out of my SKULL! If I have to wander through another forest or deal with another mangy wild animal, I'm going to SCREAM! My life is VERY stressful. The insects are annoying, and have you ever tried to get the scent of a SKUNK out of your hair? It's next to impossible! And look at the clothes we get! I've had this ugly cotton dress for the past two years. I'm just DYING to wear a velvet dress with red sparkly shoes for a day. And a Renegade's love life is nonexistent, unless you're really into the outdoorsy types."

I felt bad for Goldilocks. Although, to be honest, she sounded a lot like what I would call a dork.

"And then there are the ROGUES. A lot of them are selfish magic users obsessed with power and prestige. They have no qualms about hurting others to get ahead. And they're VAIN! They love titles like the 'Evil' this or the 'Wicked' that. Their lives are filled with danger, drama, and intrigue.

"The fairies are magic users too, but they are nice. They're responsible for keeping Fairy Tale Land in existence. Basically, we ALL just try to get along and tell our stories."

"Well, I don't know why the Wicked Witch of the West would mislead you, Goldilocks," I said solemnly. "But this place ISN'T a B AND B! And I think we need to get the HECK out of here. FAST!"

458

ME, EXPLAINING TO GOLDILOCKS
THAT WE SHOULD PROBABLY LEAVE BEFORE
THE THREE BEARS COME HOME!!

Plus, I'm also SUPERallergic to very hungry BEARS!

Suddenly we heard a loud, angry growl from the kitchen.

"Somebody's been EATING my porridge!!" roared Papa Bear.

"Somebody's been eating MY porridge too!!" snarled Mama Bear.

"Somebody's been eating MY porridge! And they ate it all up!" wailed Baby Bear.

Goldilocks and I just froze and stared at each other in horror! The bears were back home! ☹!! Next, the loud, angry growl was even CLOSER to us, from the living room.

"Somebody's been SITTING in my chair!" roared Papa Bear.

"Somebody's been sitting in MY chair too," snarled Mama Bear.

"And somebody sat in MY chair and broke it into pieces!" sobbed Baby Bear.

"Alice, what are we going to do?" Goldilocks whisper-shouted. "I haven't yet taken the class Angry Animals with Very Sharp Teeth: Up Close and Personal!"

"Well, um . . . we can always hide?" I said, shrugging.

"Where?!! Under THIS bed?!! That's the FIRST place they are going to look for us!" Goldilocks said, rolling her eyes.

"YES! Under the bed!" I whispered. "We don't have a choice!"

We quickly straightened Baby Bear's bed so it wouldn't be obvious that someone had been sleeping in it. That's when I realized in horror that I had accidentally dropped some of my personal belongings on the bed.

Goldilocks pointed and motioned frantically, but it was TOO late for me to try to retrieve my stuff.

We were DOOMED 😟! Goldilocks and I quickly dove under the bed. And when we cautiously peeked out, the bear family was standing in the bedroom just inches away from our hiding place. . . .

GOLDILOCKS AND ME,
PEEKING OUT FROM UNDER THE BED!!

"Somebody's been SLEEPING in my bed!!" roared Papa Bear.

"Somebody's been sleeping in MY bed too!!" snarled Mama Bear.

"Somebody's been sleeping in MY bed!" cried Baby Bear. Then he pointed excitedly. "Mama Bear! Papa Bear! Look what's STILL there!!"

Baby Bear's cute little fuzzy toes were so close that his fur was actually tickling my nose. OMG! I was trying my hardest NOT to SNEEZE! I was like, AH! AH! AH! CH—!

That's when Goldilocks quickly reached over and grabbed the end of my nose. The good news was that she stopped my sneeze ☺! The bad news was that the pressure from NOT sneezing almost ruptured my eyeballs! OUCH ☹!!

The bears froze and just STARED at the bed!

"Well, look at that!" bellowed Papa Bear.

463

"Unbelievable!" shouted Mama Bear.

"LET'S EAT THEM!!" cried Baby Bear.

This is what the Three Bears found. . . .

THE THREE BEARS, FINDING MY YUMMY
STASH OF NUTS, BERRIES, AND FRUIT!

"I have a great idea, Papa Bear!" cooed Mama Bear. "Why don't you and Baby Bear go fix that broken chair while I warm up our porridge and bake us a delicious apple blueberry pie with a honey nut glaze!!" she gushed.

Then all three bears happily lumbered back into the kitchen and got busy with their chores.

As soon as the coast was clear (and the bears were greedily snarfing down a yummy pie), Goldilocks and I climbed out of a window and disappeared into the woods.

I can't really explain it, but for some reason I really like her, even though she's kind of ditzy.

Maybe it's because she looks and acts so much like my BFF Chloe. Minus the curly blond hair.

I'm STILL pretty anxious to go home. But I also want to know more about the ROGUES.

One of them obviously tried to set up my new friend, Chloelocks! Er . . . I mean, GOLDILOCKS!

Thank goodness those bears decided to eat Mama Bear's freshly baked PIE as a midday snack instead of GOLDILOCKS!

YIKES!!

SOMEONE wants Goldilocks DEAD! And that someone is MacKenzie, the Wicked Witch of the West!

I can't even take a wacky trip to Fairy Tale Land without that girl showing up and making my life miserable.

And I'm SURE she's plotting some over-the-top diabolical plan! Which means the Munchkins, Goldilocks, and all of Fairy Tale Land might possibly be in great danger.

And since I'm basically STUCK here in ~~Fairy Tale Land~~ Cray-Cray Land for the time being, I don't have a choice but to try to stop her.

BACK INTO THE WOODS!

Goldilocks and I quickly became friends. I told her my story and explained that I was desperately trying to get back home.

Although she personally didn't know the Wizard of Odd, she volunteered to help me find him. Of course I was REALLY happy to hear that news! Goldilocks said it was the least she could do after I had saved her life.

However, first she had to file an incident report with the Fairy Tale Land Council about the Three Bears.

She also explained that a powerful magic user had recently begun interfering with fairy tales and that the Fairy Tale Land Council wanted the person stopped before serious damage was done.

We agreed to meet in one hour at a place called the Mad Hatter Tea Shop. It was located in a small village at the edge of the forest about a mile away.

I had been on the path for about fifteen minutes when I noticed a figure ahead of me in the distance. It was a girl, and she was wearing a bright red cape with a hood and carrying a small basket.

Maybe she knew the Wizard of Odd. I figured it wouldn't hurt to ask.

I took off, running after her as fast as I could. But soon she disappeared into a small cottage.

I was like, JUST GREAT ☹!!

Trespassing on private property was fast becoming a dangerous new hobby of mine. I had barely survived the run-in with the bear family.

However, since it was kind of an emergency, I decided to go inside.

When I finally got a glimpse of the girl, I couldn't believe my eyes! She looked just like my BFF ZOEY!! . . .

Well, okay. IF Zoey was wearing a funky red cape, a retro dress, cool ankle boots, and was carrying a cute wicker basket handbag.

469

Apparently, the girl was visiting her grandmother.

But then their convo got really . . . um, WEIRD!!

Even weirder than the chats between ME and MY grandmother (which are usually pretty weird!).

"Grandma, what big EYES you have!"

"The better to SEE you with, my dear."

"Grandma, what big EARS you have!"

"The better to HEAR you with, my dear."

Anyway, it was quite obvious that Red Riding Hood needed glasses or something, because her GRANDMA looked like no grandma I'd ever seen before.

I don't mean to be rude or impolite, but her grandma was definitely a bit on the homely side.

Okay, I'll be honest. She was a HOT MESS!! . . .

ME, NOTICING THAT GRANDMA
NEEDED TO SHAVE . . . HER ENTIRE BODY!!

"Grandma, what a big NOSE you have!"

"The better to SMELL you with, my dear!"

"Grandma, what big TEETH you have!"

"The better to EAT you with!! GRRRRR!!!"

And with that, the wolf leaped across the bed, right at Red Riding Hood.

Okay, I knew there was supposed to be a huntsman or some guy who shows up at the last minute to save the day in the fairy tale. But he was nowhere in sight.

"Fairy Godmother! Please HELP!" I screamed, praying she would appear. But no luck.

Snarling and gnashing his sharp teeth, that wolf darted right past the door I was hiding behind.

He was about to pounce on poor, helpless Red Riding Hood and rip her to shreds. . . .

THE BIG BAD WOLF, POUNCING ON
POOR RED RIDING HOOD!

That's when I completely PANICKED and did the
first (STUPID) thing that popped into my head. . . .

ME, GRABBING THE WOLF'S TAIL
AND PULLING IT WITH ALL MY MIGHT
IN A DESPERATE ATTEMPT TO SAVE
RED RIDING HOOD!!

But I guess I must have pulled a little too hard or something, because I heard a loud *SNAP*, and then . . .

ME AND THE WOLF, FALLING OVER
WHEN HIS TAIL SNAPS OFF!

ME AND THE WOLF,
BOTH VERY SHOCKED AND SURPRISED
THAT HIS TAIL WAS IN MY HAND ☹!

Of course, after the wolf got over the initial shock, he got an attitude about the whole thing. Even though it was quite obviously an accident.

"Look what you've done, you . . . you MONSTER!!" he yelled at me. "I'm lucky to have survived such a vicious attack. You're a psychopath, and you need help!"

"Oh, REALLY?! So I'M the monster here?!" I shouted at him. "Just a minute ago YOU were the one bragging about your big teeth and trying to EAT Red Riding Hood. After dressing up as her GRANDMA, no less! Sorry, dude, but YOU'RE the one who needs some SERIOUS counseling."

Then he got right up in my face, so close I could smell his foul Big Bad Wolf breath.

Suddenly I totally understood how he had huffed and puffed and blew down the houses of those poor Three Little Pigs.

OMG! His breath was THAT bad!!! ☹!!

"Listen, Dorothy, if you know what's good for you, you'll stay out of MY neck of the woods!! Or else! And that's NOT a threat, it's a PROMISE!!" he growled at me. Literally.

"I'm NOT Dorothy! And YOU'RE just a big BULLY!"

"Okay then, um . . . ALICE!! You'd better watch your step!"

"I'm NOT Alice, either!" I shot back.

"Well, you should be! You're wearing her UGLY dress. I personally wouldn't be caught DEAD in that thing, especially with those awful shoes!"

"Hey, have you looked in the mirror lately, Wolf Boy? You're wearing a granny gown with ugly flowers on it, and a matching bonnet. I wouldn't be giving out fashion advice if I were you," I huffed.

Then he rolled his eyes at me, snatched his tail out of my hand, and stomped right out the front door.

ME AND RED RIDING HOOD,
GIGGLING ABOUT THE TAIL FIASCO!

"You actually saved my life! How can I ever thank you, Dorothy?! I mean, er . . . Alice! Or whatever your name is. . . ."

I was totally surprised when she gave me a big hug.

"Here, would you like a free lunch? It's a peanut butter and jelly sandwich. Grandma—I mean, the wolf—didn't eat it."

"I'm really happy I was able to help you," I said. "And thanks for offering me lunch. But after yesterday, I'm just not that into PB and J sandwiches anymore. It's a long and complicated story. But do you know where I can get a triple cheeseburger, extra-large fries, and a supersize drink?!"

"My! What a BIG appetite YOU have!! You could be one of the Three Little Pigs!" she blurted out.

I just ignored that little comment. Something else was kind of bugging me.

"Um, why didn't you realize that the wolf WASN'T your grandma?" I asked her.

"Actually, I wasn't visiting MY grandma. I was just delivering a basket of food for the grandmother of one of the Rogues," Red Riding Hood explained.

"Well, whoever sent you here is either genetically related to the canine family or was trying to turn you into an afternoon snack. I'm really worried that someone is out to get both you and Goldilocks!"

That's when Red Riding Hood gasped and said, "Goldilocks is a good friend of mine! We're both in danger?" Then she clutched her heart and shrieked, "Oh! My! Gosh!"

Someone had actually tried to kill her, and it seemed to be FINALLY sinking in.

But then she blurted out, "MY, what big FEET you have, Dorothy! I mean, Alice!"

Of course I was highly offended by her insensitive little comment. But I figured she'd only said that because the enchanted shoes made my feet look a lot bigger or something.

Anyway, I invited Red Riding Hood to join Goldilocks and me for tea at the Mad Hatter Tea Shop.

Between the three of us, I was sure we'd find that Wizard of Odd guy.

And he'd be able to help me get back home.

☺!!

THE MAD HATTER TEA SHOP

Red Riding Hood and I met Goldilocks at the Mad Hatter Tea Shop, a quaint little café at the edge of the woods.

It was owned by a friendly but eccentric guy, called the Mad Hatter due to his large collection of wacky-looking hats.

When he came to our table to take our order, I couldn't help but stare in shock.

First of all, he had a pet mouse that he carried around on a small tray, and—get this—they were wearing matching jackets. (Which, BTW, also shed light on his name, because obviously this guy was a little . . . um, MAD!)

And second, he looked just like my good friend Theodore Swagmire III! Which was not all that surprising, considering the fact that practically EVERYONE in Fairy Tale Land looked just like someone I knew from home. . . .

GOLDILOCKS AND RED RIDING HOOD,
STARING IN DISBELIEF AT THE MOUSE,
WHILE I STARE AT THE MAD HATTER,
WHO LOOKS LIKE THEO SWAGMIRE!

"Welcome to the Mad Hatter Tea Shop, ladies! May I have your order, please?" he said.

"Hi there!" I said. "I'd like lemon tea with honey, and the sunshine lemon cookies, please!"

"Okay! And for you, miss?" he said, looking at Goldilocks.

"Well, I'd like the raspberry tea. But not too hot! And not too cold, either! I think lukewarm would be just right. And, let's see, the peanut butter crunch cookies are too hard. But the old—fashioned tea cookies are too soft. The cinnamon doodles are probably too spicy, and the vanilla wafers too bland. So I think I'll take the chocolate chip cookies! They'll be just right!"

"That sounds good! And now for you, miss?" he said, nodding to Red Riding Hood.

"Well, I have a few things I'd like to discuss before I place my order," Red Riding Hood said.

"Of course. Go right ahead!" The Mad Hatter smiled.

"Well, I couldn't help noticing what a BIG hat you have!"

"Yes, it's my favorite color—green. It was an unbirthday gift from my sister."

"And what a CUTE little mouse you have!"

"I've had him since I was a child. He goes everywhere with me. He loves to nibble on cheese and strawberries."

"Okay, and what a FANCY teapot you have!"

"Thank you! It belonged to my grandmother. I love her dearly. She's as sweet as sugar!"

I was starting to wonder how long Red Riding Hood planned to interrogate the Mad Hatter. But then she nodded her head and smiled.

"Thank you for your comments! I'll have the green tea with extra sugar and the strawberry cheesecake cookies."

OMG!

Our tea and cookies were DELISH! . . .

GOLDILOCKS, RED RIDING HOOD,
AND ME, HAVING A SUPERFUN
TEA PARTY!

Just as we were finishing up, three girls came into the tea shop, accompanied by two royal escorts and five royal guards. . . .

They wore beautiful dresses and the finest jewelry and shoes.

When they spotted Goldilocks and Red Riding Hood, they immediately rushed over and gave them hugs and air kisses.

I was SUPERexcited when Goldilocks introduced me to them. "Rapunzel, Snow White, and Sleeping Beauty, I'd like you to meet my new friend . . ."

That's when I noticed that Rapunzel looked like my friend Marcy, Snow White looked like my friend Violet, and Sleeping Beauty looked like my friend Jenny. I couldn't stop staring at them.

Goldilocks continued. "Her name is—"

"DOROTHY!" the three girls squealed in unison.

"I'd know that dress anywhere," cried Rapunzel.

"Um, no! She's NOT Dorothy," said Goldilocks. "Her name is—"

"ALICE!" the three girls squealed in unison again.

"That dress is a dead giveaway!" said Snow White.

"Sorry, guys! I know the blue dress and white apron are kind of confusing. But my name is Nikki. It's really nice to meet all of you."

The three girls looked at me, then each other, and then me again.

"Hi, Nikki!" said Sleeping Beauty. "We don't recognize your face. What fairy tale are you in?"

"Actually, NONE!"

"Really?" said Rapunzel, with a puzzled look on her face. "That's very strange. EVERYONE in Fairy Tale Land has a story! Have you filed a report with the Fairy Tale Land Council yet? They are supposed to assign you a story within forty-eight hours."

"Yeah, it's pretty simple," said Snow White. "You just tell them if you're Regal, Renegade, or Rogue, and they'll hook you up."

"Well, actually, I'm none of those," I explained.
"I ended up here due to a freak accident, and I'm
trying to get home. I've been wandering in the woods
for almost two days now. So it's quite obvious I'm—"

"RENEGADE!" the three girls excitedly squealed.

"Definitely!" said Rapunzel.

"For sure!" said Snow White.

"Totally!" said Sleeping Beauty.

"LOST!" I said, starting to get a little irritated.
"It's quite obvious I'm LOST!" But I understood why
those girls said that, seeing as I was wandering in
the woods and all.

"Nikki, you are SO lucky!" Rapunzel gushed. "At least
you have your independence and get treated like a
young adult. When I'm not locked away in some stupid
tower going STIR-CRAZY, I can't go anywhere without
a royal escort. Why do I need a highly paid babysitter?!
And just look at me! Every day is a BAD HAIR day!

I'd love to get a SUPERcute short haircut, but instead I'm dragging around an eighteen-foot-long braid. Do you have any idea how long it takes me to wash and blow-dry my hair? Nineteen hours! I'm a teenager, but I spend most of my time taking care of my hair."

"Don't get me started!" Sleeping Beauty griped. "Our lives are micromanaged by kings, queens, princes, and even witches we've never met before. We're told to do this! Do that! Bite the apple! Prick your finger! Fall asleep! Wake up! Let down your hair! We're really SICK and TIRED of being bossed around. Personally, I'd much rather live in a cute little gingerbread house than a huge, drafty castle. And on Saturday mornings I just wanna sleep in for a few hours. NOT for a HUNDRED YEARS!!! Like, WHO does THAT?!!"

"I'd trade places with you guys in a heartbeat," Snow White fumed. "We're tired of kissing princes, kissing frogs, and kissing seven dwarfs. And if I'm FORCED to attend one more BORING party, I'm going to punch someone! How about a little 'me time'? I'd give anything just to chill out alone in the peaceful woods without some evil hag trying to poison me with an apple!"

Red Riding Hood, Goldilocks, and I just STARED at those girls in disbelief. Who would have guessed that life as a princess was so CRUDDY?! . . .

RAPUNZEL, SNOW WHITE, AND SLEEPING BEAUTY, COMPLAINING ABOUT HOW CRUDDY IT IS TO BE A PRINCESS!

So the Regals thought the Renegades had perfect lives. And the Renegades thought the Regals had perfect lives.

And I'm guessing that some of the Rogues probably felt the same way too.

It appeared that everybody thought everyone else had the PERFECT life. Go figure!

That's when a little lightbulb popped on in my head and I got the most BRILLIANT idea!

"Listen up! If all of you are so unhappy with the way things are, why don't you just change things up a bit?"

"WHAT?!" all five of them gasped.

"Why can't you guys just swap stories or maybe even share them? It sounds like you Renegades would love to go to a party or soak in a bubble bath. And it sounds like you Regals would love to chill out in the woods or go on an adventure. So just do it!"

That's when all five girls started squealing happily and jumping up and down in excitement.

They LOVED my idea!

"What about the Fairy Tale Land Council?" Sleeping Beauty asked. "There are really strict rules about which characters go in which fairy tales. We could get in big trouble!"

"What does it matter, as long as the story is told?" Red Riding Hood said.

"Besides, how will they know?! It will be OUR secret!" Snow White added.

"Well, once the Council sees that the new way of doing things actually works AND everyone is happier, I'm sure they'll come around," I reasoned.

I had a really good feeling that very soon Fairy Tale Land was going to be a much better place! The six of us did a group hug with me in the middle to celebrate a bright and exciting new future. . . .

THE REGALS, THE RENEGADES, AND ME,
DOING A GROUP HUG!!

"Thank you for helping US, Nikki. But NOW we need to help YOU get back home!" said Red Riding Hood.

"Well, my fairy godmother suggested the Wizard of Odd," I said. "But I haven't been able to find him."

"Wait a minute!" Sleeping Beauty yawned excitedly. "Every year the wizard attends the Spring Ball given by King and Queen Charming at their castle. And guess what? I think it's TONIGHT!"

"You're right!" Snow White said. "It's by special invitation to Regals only. But since we're so tired of the royal party scene, we didn't RSVP. So, unfortunately, we're NOT on the guest list. But maybe we can try to SNEAK you in!"

"No! That would be way too dangerous!" I said. "The last thing I want is to risk any of you getting caught and punished for helping me! I'll just have to do this on my own."

After much debate, all five girls reluctantly agreed with me.

We said our good-byes, and then I began the two-mile journey to the Northern Kingdom, which was ruled by King and Queen Charming.

I didn't have any idea how I would get inside the castle to attend the ball. And even if I did, what was the likelihood I'd convince the Wizard of Odd to help me, a total stranger?

The chances of my plan actually working were slim to none.

But if I had any hope of ever returning home, failure was NOT an option!

☹!!

PUMPKINS AND MICE

When I finally reached the Charming Castle in the Northern Kingdom, the royal ball had already begun.

The cream-colored stone castle was even more magnificent than I had imagined. It had seven huge towers with colorful tiled roofs that glistened like jewels in the setting sun.

A least three dozen royal guards stood watch outside on the palace grounds.

Trying to sneak past those guys was going to be next to impossible. I must have looked really suspicious or something, because one of them marched right over and glared at me.

"Excuse me, missy! But the royal ball is by invitation only. So please move along. I don't want to have to arrest you for loitering or trespassing on royal property!" he barked.

OMG! I'd recognize that scowl anywhere.

It was Mr. Grumpy, the security guard from the Bad Boyz concert! But his ID badge said Sir Grumpy of the 5th Royal Battalion.

The last thing I needed right then was to get arrested by an overzealous royal guard. So, I quickly retreated down the castle walkway. And when no one was looking, I ducked inside an open door of the royal horse stables and hid in an empty stall.

I flopped down on a bale of hay and blinked back tears of frustration. If there was ever a time I needed a fairy godmother, this was it.

"BRIANNA! Please help! This is an emergency!" I whisper-shouted in desperation.

I held my breath and waited. But no Brianna!

However, I did manage to get the attention of three horses in neighboring stalls, who stared at me curiously.

I had been hiding in that stall for a couple of hours and must have inadvertently dozed off or something. Because the next thing I knew, someone was tapping me lightly on the shoulder.

I immediately panicked! I thought for sure Sir Grumpy had discovered my hiding place and was about to place me under arrest for trespassing on royal property.

But when I opened my eyes, a smiling face with twinkling eyes was two inches from my nose. . . .

ME, SHOCKED AND SURPRISED
BY AN UNEXPECTED VISITOR!!

I blinked a few times, and when my eyes finally came
into focus, I saw it was Brianna, my fairy godmother!

"OMG! Brianna!" I gawked at her. "Where have
you been?"

"Sorry I'm late! I got stuck in traffic," she quipped.

"Thank goodness you're here!" I said.

She checked her watch. "Well, I'll be a toothless tooth fairy! It's almost eleven o'clock!" she exclaimed. "We have get you to that royal ball before midnight!"

"Okay! Glam me up!" I cried eagerly. "And just in case there's a cute prince, I want the dress to be short . . . but not that short. And sparkly . . . but not too sparkly. And . . ."

"Shush! I'm the professional here!" Brianna said, looking annoyed. "Just let me do my job!"

"Sorry! I'm just so anxious," I said. "Go ahead."

"Thank you!" Brianna replied as she raised her magic wand and chanted: "Alakazoo! Alakazam! I want a dress that's totally glam!"

With a puff of smoke, I was transformed. I looked down at my dress and gasped. . . .

503

ME, IN SHOCK BECAUSE MY DRESS
IS MOSTLY MADE OF HAM

I was dressed head to toe in ham and assorted deli meats. My earrings and bracelets were made out of meatballs.

"Umm . . . I feel like I should be served on bread with mayo," I said.

"No, you stupid wand! I said GLAM, not HAM!" Brianna scolded it.

"So, um . . . is this the dress I'll be wearing?" I asked.

"Wait a minute. OH! Here's the problem." Brianna laughed uncomfortably. "I forgot to turn on the voice recognition."

She fidgeted with the wand and then spoke into it, "Testing! Testing! One, two, three! Is this thing on?!"

"Okeydokey! Let's try this again!" Brianna said. "Blah, blah, blah, we want a dress that's totally glam!"

POOF!!

"That's more like it! Not to brag, but this dress is MAGNIFICENT!" Brianna bragged. "So, what do you think of your new look? Oh, wait. You need a mirror!"

POOF!

Brianna zapped up a mirror.

I gazed at myself and gasped.

"Wow! I look gorgeous!"

I twirled around in my dress. "Thank you!"

"No prob. But we have to hurry! I still have to whip up your horse and carriage!"

Outside the back door of the stable was a small mouse nibbling on a pumpkin.

"PERFECT!" Brianna exclaimed. "Now stand back and be amazed at my awesome power!"

POOF!!

That spell did NOT go so well! . . .

ME, TOTALLY NOT IMPRESSED WITH MY NEW
HORSE AND CARRIAGE!

OMG! Brianna was SO embarrassed!

"Don't worry, Brianna!" I said, trying to make her
feel better. "Actually, the castle is just around the
corner. I really don't need a horse and carriage."

"Are you sure? I probably just need to make a few minor adjustments to my wand."

"Actually, I can just walk. I need the exercise!"

"Great idea!" Brianna said, and tossed the pumpkin pie and mouse over her shoulder. "Besides, one can never get too much exercise!"

I grabbed Brianna and gave her a big hug! "I really, really appreciate all of this. I'm going to find the Wizard of Odd, and he'll have me back home in no time!" I said excitedly.

"Say hello to the king and queen for me! Oh! And remember, the enchantment wears off at midnight, when the clock strikes—"

"Twelve! Yeah! I know the story!" I interrupted. "Thanks again, and good-bye!"

Then I ran toward the castle entrance as fast as my glass slippers would carry me. ☺!!

AT THE ROYAL BALL

I could hardly believe that I was actually going to a ball at the Charming Castle!

Even though my main goal was to find the Wizard of Odd, the thought of hanging out with royalty was SUPERexciting.

As I approached the main entrance, all the guards snapped to attention.

That's when I suddenly remembered that I DIDN'T have an invitation. Which meant there was still a chance I'd be arrested on the spot for trespassing on royal property. Just great ☹!!

I took a deep breath and quickly walked past the guards stationed at the huge doors, all while ~~Mr.~~ Sir Grumpy eyed me suspiciously.

As I entered the ballroom, approximately three hundred guests, dressed in the finest attire, stared at me, pointed, and whispered. . . .

ME, MAKING MY GRAND ENTRANCE
INTO THE BALLROOM

The gigantic ballroom was even more beautiful than I had imagined. It had a towering staircase with white marble floors.

Beautiful tapestries lined the walls, and two huge chandeliers hung in the center of the room, lit with dozens of candles. The royal orchestra played a waltz.

I had been wandering around the room for ten minutes, trying to find a middle-aged guy who could possibly be the wizard, when a young man approached me.

"Excuse me, miss. But I would be most honored if I could have this dance!"

OMG! I almost fainted right there on the spot!

I was gazing into the beautiful brown eyes of a dashing, princely version of BRANDON ROBERTS!

As he reached for my hand, I smiled nervously and blushed profusely. Just like I ALWAYS do when I'm around my crush, Brandon. . . .

ME, FREAKING OUT THAT BRANDON
ASKED ME TO DANCE!!

"I'm Prince Brandon. It's nice to meet you."

"Hello, I—I'm, um . . . Nikki," I stammered.

"Welcome to the Charming Castle, Princess Nikki."
He smiled. "So, where are you from?"

I could NOT believe Brandon had just called me
Princess Nikki! It was like I was in a fairy tale or
something.

Wait! I WAS in a real fairy tale! SQUEEEE ☺!!

"Well, I'm not from your world . . . er, I mean, your
kingdom," I answered.

"So, what brings you here, Your Highness? Are you
visiting family or friends?"

"Actually, I'm looking for someone. It's a very
important personal matter. Maybe you know him?"

Disappointment flashed across Brandon's face.
"So, have your parents arranged your marriage?

If so, I wish you both the best. He's a very lucky guy."

"NO! It's NOT like that at all!" I giggled. "I'm looking for the Wizard of Odd."

"Really! The Wizard of Odd? May I ask why?"

"It's regarding, um . . . my travel arrangements. Back to my . . . kingdom. I was told he would be here tonight," I said, glancing around the room again.

"Actually, he's an acquaintance of my parents. I think they said he was called away on an important matter for the Queen of Hearts."

"So the wizard ISN'T here?" I asked, trying to hide my disappointment.

"No. But if it's important for you to see him, perhaps I could escort you to the Queen of Hearts' castle. I'll have the royal guards arrange a carriage whenever you're ready. It's just two miles west of here," Brandon said, staring at me intently.

I really appreciated Prince Brandon's offer. But if/when Sir Grumpy figured out who I really was, HE'D escort me, all right . . . straight to the royal dungeon for trespassing!

The last thing I wanted was for Prince Brandon to get into trouble trying to help ME.

"Thank you! I really appreciate your generous offer, but that won't be necessary," I said. "If it's just a few miles, I can walk."

Brandon narrowed his eyes at me. "WALK?! Alone?! In the forest?! Are you sure? Most princesses would never consider doing such a thing."

"Hanging out in the forest can be pretty exciting!" I smiled. "Well, during the daytime, anyway!"

"Well, if you change your mind, just let me know. I could use a little excitement in MY life." He sighed. "There's so much to explore outside these palace walls. But that's impossible to do when I'm always escorted by eight royal guards. My parents insist on it! I'm bored silly of my mundane princely duties!"

"What? No white horse, shining armor, epic quests, or damsels in distress?!" I teased.

"Only Renegades have the freedom to be real heroes. I'd give anything to be one for just a day. Instead, I'm CHASED by screaming fangirls and STALKED by prince-obsessed witches wanting to turn me into a frog!"

"A FROG?!" I snickered. "So, is that where the saying 'You have to kiss a lot of frogs to find your prince' comes from?!"

BRANDON, AS AN ADORABLE FROG?!!

"Hey, that's NOT funny!" Brandon deadpanned. "And to make matters worse, the only things my friends like to do are hang out at my castle, play polo, and party."

"Well, Prince Brandon, it sounds to me like you need to find some NEW friends!" I joked.

"That's great advice. Then it's settled. YOU, Princess Nikki, shall be my NEW best friend!" Brandon winked.

"Well, your new best friend thinks you'd make an AWESOME hero!" I gushed. "You should follow your dreams!"

"I really want to," he said, with a worried look on his face. "But what will my parents say?"

"They'll say they're proud of you! Just go for it!"

The apprehension on his face melted into an encouraged smile.

"I think you're the first person who totally understands me, Princess Nikki! Even though we've just met, you feel like a trusted friend. It's as if I've known you in another life."

"You do! Er . . . I mean, you do . . . seem like a nice guy!"

That's when he smiled and stared at me, and I smiled and stared back at him.

All of this smiling and staring went on for what seemed like FOREVER!

The music started up again, and Brandon took my hand and led me onto the dance floor.

OMG!

Dancing with him was SO romantic. . . .

Practically everyone in the room was staring at us and probably wondering who I was.

PRINCE BRANDON AND ME, DANCING!

We danced and laughed and talked. I wanted the night to last forever.

"I've never met anyone quite like you, Princess Nikki. You're VERY . . . different!" Brandon said.

"Is that a bad thing?" I asked.

"You're smart, funny, and adventurous! I really like you! So, can I see you again? I'll travel to your kingdom, no matter how far away it is."

"I'd love to see you again too!" I gushed. "But, unfortunately, I don't think that's possible!"

"ANYTHING is possible, Your Highness!"

That's when Prince Brandon gazed so deeply into my eyes that my heart skipped a beat!

Squeee!!

Then he leaned in for the perfect fairy tale KISS and . . .

BONG!! BONG!! BONG!! . . .

ME, TOTALLY FREAKING OUT
BECAUSE IT'S MIDNIGHT!!

Our perfect fairy tale kiss was rudely interrupted!

"OMG! It's midnight already?" I cried.

I needed to get out of there quick, before I turned back into . . . well, MYSELF!

"Is something wrong?" Brandon asked, concerned.

"Um . . . YES!! I mean, NO?! It's just that . . . I really need to be going!"

"WHAT?! But the ball isn't over yet!"

"I know! But I have to go now! It's kind of an . . . emergency!"

Prince Brandon looked surprised and hurt. "I don't understand. Did I say something wrong?"

"No! I wish I could explain, but I can't! I'm really sorry!"

"Princess Nikki! Please! Don't go!"

"It was nice meeting you! Good-bye!!"

"But when will I see you again? I NEED to see you again!" Brandon pleaded. "Please! Will you at least tell me where you live?"

It seems like whenever things are perfect in my life, disaster swoops in like a pigeon with a bad case of diarrhea and poops on my head!

Even though I knew the "Cinderella" story line, I was still pretty upset at the turn of events.

Hey! It wasn't just ANY prince I was DITCHING at the ball!

It was my crush, BRANDON! Right in the middle of a KISS ☹!!

BONG! BONG! BONG! The clock continued to chime.

I turned and hurried across the dance floor and up the grand staircase. . . .

ME, VERY RUDELY DITCHING
PRINCE BRANDON AT THE BALL!!

If you've ever worn heels before, you know that running in those things will almost always guarantee a TRIP to the hospital.

No pun intended!

Lucky for me, I only lost a shoe. Just like in the fairy tale.

As I rushed toward the door, once again the entire ballroom was staring at me, pointing, and whispering.

I was like, JUST GREAT ☹!!

I felt horrible about leaving Prince Brandon at the ball like that! But I didn't have a choice. Or did I?

What girl wouldn't want to be a princess, marry a handsome prince, and live happily ever after?!

I hesitated at the door just for a second and took one final glance over my shoulder. . . .

I felt so sorry for Brandon. And SO confused!!

But he deserved a REAL princess.

Not a FAKE, wannabe princess like ME!

I sighed deeply and was suddenly overcome by a wave of sadness. Then I turned and rushed out the door.

I barely made it past the royal guards as the magical enchantment started to wear off.

Now back in my own clothing, I ducked into the royal stables and made my way to my hiding place in the back stall. I was so mentally and physically exhausted from the night's adventures that I didn't even mind sleeping on the scratchy, smelly hay.

Tomorrow I was going to make the journey to the Queen of Hearts' castle. And once there, I'd convince the Wizard of Odd to help me get back home.

I tried to sleep, but all I could think of was Prince Brandon and the crushed look on his face. I was the CRUELEST person ever!!

Overwhelmed by guilt and remorse, I cried myself to sleep.

AT THE QUEEN OF HEARTS' CASTLE

I got up bright and early and began my journey to the Queen of Hearts' castle. I was desperately praying that the wizard would still be there.

I still feel pretty awful about ditching Prince Brandon at the ball. He's such a nice guy.

But the perfect girl for him is out there somewhere. And I'm pretty sure she isn't ME.

Right now my major goal in life is to find my way back home. So starting a relationship with a very cute prince in Fairy Tale Land would only complicate things.

Besides, most of the time I'm totally overwhelmed dealing with just ONE Brandon!

HOW would I ever handle TWO of him?!

Anyway, before I knew it, I found myself standing right outside the Queen of Hearts' castle. . . .

THE QUEEN OF HEARTS' CASTLE!!

It was quite obvious that the queen was totally OBSESSED with hearts! I saw dozens of them! She even had heart-shaped doors and windows. A group of guards marched back and forth in formation at the main entrance. After a few minutes I finally summoned up the courage to approach one of them.

"Excuse me, sir. But I was wondering if it would be possible for me to speak with the—"

"What are you doing out here, missy? Haven't you heard? The Queen of Hearts has decreed a state of emergency! A very dangerous and powerful magic user is terrorizing our citizenry and plans to overthrow Her Royal Highness the Queen. The entire kingdom is on high alert!"

"Wow! I wasn't aware of that! Is the magic user named MacKenzie?" I asked, mostly out of curiosity. "I heard the Munchkins complaining that she'd been harrassing them for quite a while."

"You actually KNOW this diabolical perpetrator?!" he practically shouted as he excitedly summoned the other guards.

"Um . . . no! Actually, I DON'T know for sure WHO the person is. I was j—just asking," I stammered.

"Well, the queen is offering a handsome reward for any information leading to the capture of this heinous criminal. And she's ordered the most powerful magic user in the land to apprehend the person. I think it would be a good idea for you to speak with him. Now come along, please."

"I really wish I could help you. But I'm supposed to be leaving the kingdom very soon. Like, any minute now. I'm really sorry!" I said as I tried to walk away.

But the guards quickly surrounded me.

"It's urgent that you report to the Wizard of Odd for questioning. Please follow me, young lady! GUARDS! FALL IN! FORWARD, MARCH!"

I could not believe my ears! I was being escorted into the castle to see the wizard!! SQUEEEEE ☺!!!

My dream had come true! Because standing inside
the great hall was the man himself. . . .

THE GREAT WIZARD OF ODD!!!

I have to admit, I was a little shocked and surprised to see that he looked just like Principal Winston from my middle school.

But hey!

I didn't care if he looked like a two-headed lizard with three eyes, a mustache, and a bad hair weave!!

I was finally going HOME! SQUEEEEE ☺!

I was SO happy, I wanted to cry!

"Hello, Mr. Wizard, sir! I've been searching for you for FOREVER! My name is Nikki Maxwell! And I was wondering if you would PLEASE, PLEASE help me go ho—"

That's when his smile immediately vanished. He narrowed his eyes at me and scowled.

"Did you just say your name is Nikki Maxwell?!" he bellowed.

"Um, y—yes?" I squeaked nervously. The wizard quickly pulled a large scroll from his robe pocket and opened it.

Then he started reading overdramatically in a booming voice, "Nikki Maxwell, Most Wicked Witch of the Unknown Kingdom! By order of the Queen of Hearts, I demand that you cease and desist terrorizing the citizenry of this humble kingdom with your dark and evil magic. Are you prepared to stand before your accusers?"

I didn't have the slightest idea what that guy was talking about. I WASN'T a wicked witch! This had to be some kind of mistake.

"My accusers?! What accusers?!" I sputtered.

"Guards! Bring in the accusers!" the wizard ordered.

A small group was ushered in and stood there GLARING at me. . . .

I FINALLY MEET MY ACCUSERS!

I was a little freaked out when I first saw the Queen of Hearts. She looked suspiciously like the celebrity figure skater Victoria Steel from my *Holiday on Ice* charity show back in December.

A cold shiver went down my spine. That lady was VAIN, MEAN, and CRAZY!!

The rest of the group included:

1. MacKenzie—Okay, so she was probably still VERY ticked off about the fact that I'd landed on her upon my arrival in Fairy Tale Land. And yes! I was STILL wearing HER magical sneakers (which she hopefully didn't realize because they had changed into a cute pair of black Mary Janes).

2. The Wolf—He was STILL dressed in a granny gown and obviously STILL had an attitude about the whole broken tail thing. Which, BTW, was TOTALLY an accident!

3. The Bear Family—Yes, my friend Goldilocks had pretty much trashed their house AND eaten their

porridge. So I completely understood why they were still a little upset. But I had left them a very yummy snack of nuts and berries. Didn't I get any credit for THAT good deed?!

Suddenly MacKenzie walked up to me, stuck her finger right in my face, and screeched, "YES! That's HER! She tried to brutally murder me! And I think she stole my designer sneakers and is hiding them! She's a very powerful and evil magic user with plans to dispose of the wizard and take over the Queen of Hearts' castle and kingdom. I overheard her bragging about it to the Munchkins! Although she looks innocent and stupid, don't trust her for one second!"

I could NOT believe MacKenzie was LYING about me like that right in front of my FACE!! No wonder everyone was ~~mad~~ even MADDER at me.

"There's been an awful mistake! I didn't do any of those terrible things! Well, okay. Maybe I did a few of them! But some of that stuff was totally by accident. Please, Your Highness. I beg of you! Please do something! Anything!" I cried.

And she did! The Queen of Hearts pointed at me and screamed . . .

"OFF WITH YOUR HEAD!!!"

Then she ordered me to stand trial for my crimes against the kingdom tomorrow at sunrise!!

JUST GREAT ☹!!

That's when MacKenzie came over and gave me a big hug!

"You poor thing! I feel SO bad for you! But, the most important thing is to just stay calm through all of this and NOT lose your head! Oops! Did I just say 'lose your head'? SORRY!"

Then she sashayed away! I just HATE it when MacKenzie sashays.

Anyway, I tried to look on the bright side. I was very sure that by tomorrow the queen would realize she had made a HUGE mistake.

And if I actually did have a trial, there was no doubt in my mind that all my new friends in Fairy Tale Land would testify that I was a decent person.

The challenge was going to be contacting everyone before my trial at sunrise.

Just as I was about to leave the castle to try to round up witnesses for my trial, the guards stopped me.

"Not so fast, Miss Wicked Witch . . . from the . . . Unknown—!"

"I am NOT a wicked witch!" I snapped.

"I have specific orders from the queen to keep you locked up until your trial and execution tomorrow! To the DUNGEON with YOU! You'll be sharing a cell with the rats!!"

"DUNGEON?!! RATS?!! EXECUTION?!!" I gasped.

Then I took a big breath and screamed with every ounce of my being. . . .

"BRIANNA!! HEEEEEEEEELLLP!!"

Unfortunately, Brianna was a no-show. AGAIN!!

Brianna was VERY lucky that the Queen of Hearts had placed me under arrest right then.

Because I would have marched right over to the Fairy Tale Land Council headquarters and filed a complaint against Brianna for "incompetent fairy godmothering" (or whatever) and demanded an immediate replacement!

Anyway, the guards escorted me down three long flights of steps, deep into the bowels of the castle.

Then they locked me in the cold, dark, dank dungeon!!

As I sat on a hard wooden bench, shivering beneath a dirty, tattered blanket, two things suddenly became quite obvious.

I was never going home, and my life was pretty much OVER!!

MY EXECUTION EVE DINNER CELEBRATION

"Get up, you lazy good-for-nothing!!" the Hawk— or in this case, Sir Hawk—yelled as he struck the dungeon bars with his sword.

CLANG! CLANG! CLANG!

I awoke from my nap, startled and confused. Even though I'd only been there five or six hours, it felt like that many days. "What's going on?" I muttered groggily.

"You're expected at the queen's Execution Eve dinner!" Sir Hawk answered as he opened the dungeon door. "Hurry up! You DON'T want to keep Her Highness waiting! She's VERY impatient!"

"Go away! I'm NOT hungry!" I grumped, and covered my head with my tattered blanket like a spoiled toddler.

"You DON'T have a choice." He scowled. "If the queen tells you to eat, you're going to EAT! Or it's OFF with your pretty little HEAD! Got it?!"

I snatched the blanket off my head and glared at that guy. Then I said . . .

"SORRY, DUDE! BUT I'M STAYING RIGHT HERE IN MY CELL! YOU CAN WAKE ME UP **AFTER** MY EXECUTION!"

Sir Hawk pulled a foot-long salami sandwich out of his boot and snarfed it down. Then he burped louder than a large moose. "This isn't a joke, pip-squeak! If I don't take you to the queen, she's going to execute ME!" he said in a quivering voice. "That lady is MEAN and SCARY!"

Even though I was the prisoner, I actually felt sorry for the guy. So I agreed to go to the queen's dinner.

I had originally planned to grab some chicken wing-dings, punch, and cake to take back to my cell. But, unfortunately, the queen had a much more elaborate evening planned for me.

I was surprised to see so many people there. They were dressed in ball gowns and tuxedos, mingling and eating hors d'oeuvres.

The queen was there too, and she was absolutely FURIOUS about something!

She pointed a finger right in my face and started screaming at me like she had lost her mind or something.

ME, HAVING AN AUDIENCE
WITH THE QUEEN OF HEARTS!

"YOU'RE LATE!!" she screamed. "Do you know how BAD you've made ME look in front of MY guests?! How am I supposed to throw an Execution Eve dinner party when the person getting executed isn't here?"

"I'm really sorry, Your Highness! I didn't mean to be late, but I was locked in your—"

"And WHY are you still in those horrible peasant rags?? Have you no SHAME?! Are you trying to embarrass me in front of my guests?!"

"I apologize! But I couldn't shop for a dress even if I wanted to," I answered, somewhat sarcastically. "I've been locked in your dungeon all day! Remember?!"

"THAT is NO excuse!" the queen shrieked. "If you RUIN my execution dinner, it's OFF WITH YOUR HEAD!! Do you understand?"

I nodded. The king, who I could have sworn was my school newspaper adviser, Mr. Zimmerman, sat nervously beside his wife.

"I don't mean to intrude, dear," the king said timidly, "but technically, you're going to execute her anyway. So . . ."

"SILENCE!!!!!!" the queen yelled.

"Yes, d-dear. Where are my manners?" the king stammered nervously. "Why don't I go get you a drink of cold punch, sweetheart?"

"Hello, world! I'm HEEEEEERE!" someone squealed.

I couldn't believe my eyes when MacKenzie sashayed into the party wearing a shimmery black chiffon witch dress and holding a diamond-encrusted gold broom.

"Don't I look stunning?" She twirled around like she was on a fashion runway. "Take it in, darlings! 'GLITCH' is the new 'glamazon'!"

I just rolled my eyes at that girl. "Glitch" was MacKenzie's cheesy slang word for a glamorous witch. . . .

MACKENZIE, THE WICKED GLITCH
("GLAM WITCH") OF THE WEST

I was like, "Sorry, girlfriend. But the only thing glitching here is your BRAIN!" But I just said that inside my head, so no one else heard it but me.

"DARLING! If it isn't the Witch of the West!" the queen exclaimed. "You look amazing, as always!" She walked away to chat with her.

I just stood there alone, scared and desperate to escape. But every exit was blocked by the queen's guards. I sighed and hung my head.

"I'm DOOMED!!" I groaned as I sadly munched on a cold, greasy duck gizzard meatball.

"PSSSSST!" I heard someone say.

I looked around, but I couldn't figure out where the sound was coming from.

"PSSSSST!" came the sound again.

I stared, dumbfounded, at a large potted plant sitting a few feet behind me. Wait! That thing wasn't there a minute ago! That's when a smiling face suddenly popped out of the leaves.

"ACK!!" I screamed. . . .

ME, FREAKING OUT WHEN A HEAD SUDDENLY POPPED OUT OF THE POTTED PLANT

"B-B-Brianna? Is that you?!" I stammered, trying to contain my happiness. . . .

ME, GIVING BRIANNA A BIG HUG!

"Yep," she answered. "You didn't think I was going to just stand by and let you get executed, did you?"

"OMG! I'm SO happy to see you!" I cried. "Please! Just get me outta here!"

"Chill out, girlfriend! Or you're gonna blow my cover!" the plant . . . er, I mean, Brianna hissed at me.

"Okay, sorry! You're a lifesaver!" I gushed. "So, what's the plan? How are you going to get me out of here?"

Brianna scratched her head with her leafy hand. "Actually . . . I haven't figured that part out. Yet!"

"I'm going to be executed in less than twelve hours, and you DON'T have a plan?!" I screeched. Quietly.

"Sorry! But I spent half a day just figuring out how to sneak into this castle. It wasn't easy coming up with such a brilliant disguise. I look like a real houseplant, don't you think?"

"Ugh! Brianna!" I groaned, SUPERannoyed. "Like I said . . . I'M DOOMED!"

"Don't be such a pessimist! Just give me some time, okay?" Brianna said. "I'll come up with a brilliant plan very soon. Trust me! But in the meantime, just try to enjoy your dinner party. You ARE the guest of honor! By the way, congratulations!"

I just rolled my eyes at that girl!

"Anyway, just keep the queen distracted for me. And whatever you do, don't mention a talking plant with pigtails," she instructed me.

"Got it!" I said, giving her a thumbs-up.

"Oh! There's one more thing . . . ," Brianna added. "And it's EXTREMELY important!"

"What do you need me to do?" I asked.

"Well . . . all this sneaking around has made me quite thirsty," she said. "Can you do me a favor and water me? About a gallon should do it."

"WATER YOU?! Brianna, I think you might be taking this plant thing a bit too seriously!"

Just then the queen's butler rang a bell, summoning everyone to the dinner table.

"Ladies and gentlemen, let the Execution Eve feast begin!" the queen declared as the crowd applauded. "Thank you all for coming. The only thing I enjoy more than watching heads roll is celebrating the joyous event with all of YOU, my loyal subjects!"

I swallowed hard and shot Brianna a terrified look. "Who says stuff like that?!" I whispered. "This woman's completely insane!"

"Forget the execution!" Brianna snarked. "You'd have to be criminally insane to decorate with all these tacky red hearts when it's not even Valentine's Day!"

I rolled my eyes at her again.

"Sorry!" she said sheepishly. "Anyway, you'd better rejoin the party before she gets mad again. We don't need her losing her temper and executing you DURING your execution celebration dinner!"

Unfortunately, as crazy as it sounded, I had to admit that Brianna was right! ☹!!

"Okay, Brianna. Good luck coming up with a rescue plan! I'll see you soon!" I said hopefully as I gave her another quick hug.

Then I turned around and bumped right into . . . MACKENZIE ☹!! OMG! I actually peed my pants!

"I've heard of tree huggers! But plant huggers?!" she snarled at me. "What's going on?"

"The experts say t-talking to p-plants helps them to g-grow?" I stammered nervously.

"GUARD! I'm allergic to creepy, sneaky plants like this one. Chop it into itty-bitty pieces and throw it into the fire! NOW!" MacKenzie screeched.

THE GUARD,
CHOPPING UP THE BRIANNA PLANT!!

I've been crying for hours, and I can't seem to stop! It's hard to believe that MacKenzie actually MURDERED my fairy godmother!

Brianna lost her life just trying to help ME! I feel so HORRIBLE right now.

I know Brianna wasn't perfect! But I wish I had been a lot nicer to her. And told her how much I appreciated her.

It's easy to take people you really care about for granted. Then, one day, they're out of your life.

Even though the Brianna plant had been chopped to pieces and burned in the fireplace, I had managed to grab a small leaf and hide it in my pocket.

It was ALL that I had left of her ☹!!

With a very heavy heart, I sadly fulfilled Brianna's last request and watered her.

With my very own TEARS!! . . .

ME, SADLY HOLDING WHAT LITTLE
WAS LEFT OF BRIANNA!

☹!!

TRIALS AND TRIBULATIONS

Today was my trial and, of course, I was pretty much freaking out ☹!! Sir Hawk placed shackles on my arms and legs and escorted me out of the dungeon. He must have felt guilty or something because he said, "I feel really sorry for you, kid. I hate my job, but I need it to keep FOOD on the table."

I stared at his big, bulging belly. I had a hard time believing he was going to die of starvation anytime soon, even if there WASN'T food on his table.

He continued. "Your trial starts in thirty minutes, and your execution is immediately afterward. They're setting up the guillotine right now!"

"GUILLOTINE!" I shrieked. "But what if I'm found INNOCENT?!"

"The Queen of Hearts is ruthless! And heartless! She'll execute you regardless of the outcome. So it won't really matter if you're innocent."

"But that's NOT fair!" I yelled. "Nobody told me I was going to be executed after my trial even if I was found innocent!"

"What do you mean? I just told you a couple of seconds ago!" Sir Hawk said, looking at me like I had the IQ of belly button lint.

Then he pulled a dozen chicken nuggets out of his helmet and popped them one by one into his mouth. He licked his fingers, burped like an ox, and sadly shook his head.

"Listen, pip-squeak. Being in the queen's justice system is like grabbing a fire-breathing dragon by the tail! Basically . . . you're TOAST!!"

I was DOOMED ☹!! My heart was pounding so hard and fast it seemed to be echoing through the dank stairwell. I gasped when MacKenzie suddenly popped out of nowhere, cackling like a, um . . . WICKED witch!

"You MURDERER!!" I screamed. "WHY?!!"

"WHY? BECAUSE I'M GOING TO BE QUEEN
OF FAIRY TALE LAND! BUT FIRST I NEED TO
DISPOSE OF YOU AND ALL THE OTHER
PESKY RENEGADES!"

"But why the Renegades?" I asked. "What did they ever do to you?"

"They're always hanging out in the woods, sticking their noses in other people's business and interfering with MY master plan!" MacKenzie complained.

"You mean by helping other people, trying to fulfill their own dreams, and making Fairy Tale Land a better place?" I asked.

"Whatever! You sound like a cheap greeting card. The Regals were bored, self-absorbed little brats until YOU came along! Now they're obsessed with becoming heroes," MacKenzie fumed. "It's DISGUSTING! And making my job a lot harder!"

"MacKenzie, YOU'RE a spoiled, self-absorbed, power-hungry little BRAT! And disgusting, too!"

"You say that like it's a BAD thing! It had taken me FOREVER, but I'd finally gotten the Regals and Renegades to hate each other. And THEMSELVES!

Then you came along and messed up everything. So now it's off with your head, girlfriend!"

"Well, if I don't stop you, I'm sure somebody will!" I said, staring right into her beady little eyes.

"Don't count on it, sweetie! The Queen of Hearts and the wizard are already my brainless pawns! And soon I'll dispose of them as well. And your silly, incompetent godmother, Brianna, made a great SALAD, don't you think?! She was NEVER a match for ME!"

When she mentioned poor Brianna, I got a big lump in my throat and blinked back my tears ☹!

MacKenzie was EVIL INCARNATE!!

But I already knew that neither the Queen of Hearts nor the wizard would believe me, even if I exposed her diabolical plan.

"Well, I'd better be going. I have a front-row seat to an execution. And I don't want to keep the queen waiting!" She giggled.

The main courtyard of the castle was packed with spectators and had an almost festive air.

At the center was a huge stage. The queen's throne sat ten feet away from a large guillotine that she had obviously designed herself.

It was heart-shaped, sprinkled with glitter, and decorated with balloons and pink and red hearts.

It was simply ADORABLE ☺!

In a very sick, dark, and demented kind of way ☹!

I took the stage and stood before her, shivering with fear.

The queen smiled and addressed the huge crowd.

"Ladies and gentlemen! Standing before you is the most vicious, cruel, and sinister person of all time. And I am NOT referring to myself! I'm talking about . . . HER!" she said, dramatically pointing at me with her scepter.

A collective gasp rose from the crowd, and a few people booed.

"As your queen, the judge, and the jury, I hereby order that Nikki Maxwell shall be immediately executed for the crime of treason and—"

The king timidly tapped the queen on her shoulder. "Excuse me for interrupting, dear. But what about the trial? To be fair, we first need to have—"

"This is MY courtroom!" she screamed. "And I can do whatever I please! Do you understand that?!"

"Yes, d-dear!" stammered the king.

"But since you insist, we'll have a trial!" she said sweetly. "The first witness I'd like to call to testify is Bud the Baker."

Surprised, Bud the Baker took the stage and stood nervously before the queen.

"So, Bud, what were you doing two days ago, while

Nikki Maxwell was so stealthily corrupting the young people of this kingdom?" the queen asked.

"Um, I dunno! All I do every day is bake," he said with a shrug. "I'm not really sure why you called me up here. I've never seen her before. . . ."

"And what do you bake?"

"Cinnamon rolls. And cupcakes, too," Bud answered.

"I LOVE cupcakes! Do you make the kind with little hearts on them? Those are my favorite!"

"Um, actually, I do," Bud answered.

"How about the ones with yummy cream filling on the inside?"

"Yes, I make those, too!"

I rolled my eyes. What did cream-filled cupcakes have to do with ME? The queen was even more insane than I had imagined.

"Now, would you bake a cream-filled heart cupcake for a ruthless criminal who was encouraging young people TO GO AGAINST THE RULES AND FOLLOW THEIR DREAMS?!!" the queen screamed at Bud the Baker.

"Um . . . well . . . I don't think that would probably be something I'd ever consider doing at the time . . . ," he babbled, overcome with fear.

"Thank you, Bud the Baker! I rest my case! Based on this testimony, I find the defendant, Nikki—"

I couldn't just stand there any longer, listening to her foolishness. So I had to rudely interrupt her.

"Your Highness, with all due respect, I OBJECT to your guilty verdict!" I said. "You're not being fair! And this trial wasn't fair! The people of this kingdom just want to be happy! And all I was trying to do was—"

"Objection OVERRULED!" the queen growled.

Then she stood up and yelled . . .

"NIKKI MAXWELL, I FIND YOU GUILTY OF
TREASON! OFF WITH YOUR HEAD!!"

Four royal guards quickly surrounded me to escort me to the guillotine for my execution.

OMG! I felt like I was going to faint!

MacKenzie was smiling insanely and waving good-bye to me.

"Now, dear! Aren't we being a bit hasty?" the king sputtered. "Surely there are witnesses who actually know what really—"

"Please, your honor! You're making a big mistake!! I beg of you, just let me explain what happened," I pleaded desperately.

"SILENCE!" screamed the Queen of Hearts. "Who among you dares to defy my order of execution?!"

It was so quiet, you could hear a pin drop.

That's when someone cleared his throat and answered, "Your Majesty, I DEFY YOU! Release the princess or answer to ME!"

I couldn't believe my eyes or my ears. Prince Brandon had come to rescue me ☺!! SQUEEE!!

"The Princess Protectors demand that you free
Nikki!" yelled three girls. It was Snow White,
Rapunzel, and Sleeping Beauty, channeling the
Three Musketeers ☺!

"Let Nikki go! Or ELSE!" shouted Goldilocks and Red Riding Hood! I couldn't help but notice they were rocking glam new makeovers!

OMG! I was SO happy to see all my friends!
And from the looks of it, they had come totally
prepared to kick some BUTT!

I frantically scanned the crowd, praying I'd see
Brianna's big, silly grin. But she WASN'T there.
I felt another rush of overwhelming sadness.

Suddenly the Queen of Hearts stood up and
bellowed, "GUARDS! APPREHEND THEM! I want
them captured alive so I can EXECUTE each and
every one of them!"

I watched in awe as the Princess Protectors and
Brandon took on a half dozen palace guards.

All three girls were joyriding on Snow White's
wheelchair with swords drawn, while Brandon pushed
them around the courtyard. They looked like an
angry three-horned bull on wheels.

When it became apparent that their side was losing,
MacKenzie and the queen tried to sneak away!

But Red Riding Hood and Goldilocks stopped them
DEAD in their tracks! . . .

"GUARD! TAKE CARE OF THESE TWO! NOW!" yelled the queen.

A burly six-foot-tall guard took one look at Red Riding Hood and Goldilocks and laughed. "You two think you're a match for ME?" he scoffed. "Cute basket! Are you gonna throw cupcakes at me? I'm really scared. So, what's in the basket, sister?"

Totally ticked off, Red Riding Hood picked up her basket and swung it at him!

POW! The man lay sprawled on the ground, howling in pain!!

"OUCH! What was in that basket? ROCKS?!!"

"No, it's the muffins she baked this morning," Goldilocks said. "They're hard as rocks! And taste like them too!"

With both girls temporarily distracted, MacKenzie ran toward me as she pulled out her wand. But Brandon saw her coming. He quickly lunged between us and threw his arms up to block her. . . .

PRINCE BRANDON, TRYING TO PROTECT ME
FROM THE WICKED WITCH OF THE WEST!!

I was really thankful that Prince Brandon had
stepped in to try to protect me from MacKenzie.
But now he had placed himself in imminent danger.

"Stand aside, Prince Brandon, or you'll be sorry!" MacKenzie threatened.

"If YOU don't back off, YOU'RE going to be sorry," he said, taking a step toward her.

"REALLY!" she sneered. "Well, aren't YOU a BRAVE little prince! But let's see how brave you are when you're green, four inches tall, and hopping around in the swamp eating FLIES!"

"NO!" I shouted. "This is between you and me, MacKenzie! I've already lost Brianna and I don't want you hurting any more innocent people!"

"Hey, I know!" she said as an evil grin spread across her face. "Why don't I turn you BOTH into frogs?! How ROMANTIC!!"

Then she pointed her wand at us. But before we could react, a bright light flashed from a wand and the room filled with mist.

And when it cleared . . .

BRIANNA (YES, BRIANNA!),
TURNING MACKENZIE INTO A FROG!!

When I saw Brianna, I was so happy that I burst into tears.

I gave her the biggest hug EVER! I never imagined that I'd ever see her alive again.

When I asked about the potted plant disguise, Brianna explained that she had quickly ditched it as soon as MacKenzie became suspicious.

The guard had just chopped up a poor houseplant, not Brianna!

Then she'd spent the rest of her time rounding up all my friends to help rescue me from the Queen of Hearts' castle!

Brianna had actually saved my life!

Soon four dozen royal guards from the Charming Kingdom arrived on the scene, and not a minute too soon.

The queen and her royal court were quickly placed

under house arrest, to be brought before King Charming and the Fairy Tale Land Council for punishment.

"Prince Brandon, WHAT are you doing HERE?" I finally asked as he flashed me a big smile.

"Well, after your inspiring pep talk about following my dreams, I decided to go on a very dangerous quest to return a priceless object to the most lovely princess in the kingdom."

"Really? How did it go?" I asked, slightly annoyed.

I didn't want to admit it, but I was feeling a little jealous of whoever this new princess was.

In spite of the time we had spent together at the ball, apparently he had already moved on to someone else.

"Well, actually, I'm not really sure yet," Prince Brandon said, staring at me with a very amused look on his face.

I personally didn't see what was so dang funny.

Then he bowed like the perfect gentleman and said . . .

"PRINCESS NIKKI,
I HAVE COURAGEOUSLY RISKED MY LIFE
FOR YOU. IT IS WITH GREAT HONOR
THAT I RETURN THIS TO
ITS RIGHTFUL OWNER."

"My glass slipper! Why, thank you, Prince Brandon!"
I giggled. "And if you don't believe shoes are
THE most important thing in life, you should ask
Cinderella. Or . . . ME!"

Everyone laughed at my silly joke. But I think Prince
Brandon and I laughed the hardest.

It was amazing to see that the Renegades and the
Regals had taken my advice. They were not only
actively pursuing their dreams, but good friends.

Everyone seemed so much happier now than when I had
first arrived. Well, almost everyone! That frog spell
Brianna cast on MacKenzie lasted twenty-four hours.

Soon it was time to say our good-byes.

Red Riding Hood, Goldilocks, Snow White, Rapunzel,
and Sleeping Beauty all gave me big hugs and
promised to come visit me in my "faraway kingdom."

Only Brandon seemed to sense the truth. That we
probably would NEVER see each other again . . .

EXCEPT IN ANOTHER LIFE!

And we were both totally fine with that.

Because EVERYONE knows that in fairy tales the prince and princess ALWAYS live . . .

HAPPILY EVER AFTER!

☺!!

STUCK IN FAIRY TALE LAND! AGAIN!

When Brianna and I met with the Fairy Tale Land
Council later that day about my trip home, we
received some very bad news. Not a single magic user
in the entire kingdom was powerful enough to send me
back to another world. Not even the Wizard of Odd!

Actually, the wizard had no magical powers
whatsoever! He was a big fake dressed up in a
fancy wizard costume, just like in the *Wonderful
Wizard of Oz* story.

I had to admit that after the fiasco with the
Queen of Hearts and the Wicked Witch of the
West, I was happy to be alive! But I still really
missed my family and friends and was heartbroken
that I'd never see them again.

I was curious when Brianna came in lugging a big
dusty book that was almost as large as she was.
The weird thing was that it looked SUPERfamiliar.

Finally I realized it was the exact same book

that my English teacher had brought to class!

"So, Nikki! Are you ready to go back home?" Brianna grinned.

"OMG! Brianna, you can send me home?!!" I screamed excitedly. "I thought you said you weren't powerful enough to do that!"

"Well, transporting a person to another world requires advanced magic. But I've been studying this book, and I think I've come up with a magic spell that should do the trick! Are you ready?"

I felt totally torn because now that I was FINALLY going home, I felt a little sad to be leaving. I gave Brianna a big hug and thanked her for saving my life!

"Okay, Nikki! Stand right here!" she instructed.

> "Magic potion, lucky charm!
> Fairy Tale Land is safe from harm!
> Nikki Maxwell saved the day!
> So send her back home right . . . um . . .

"RIGHT . . . NOW! RIGHT . . . THIS MINUTE!
UM, HOW ABOUT RIGHT . . . HANDED?"

Brianna giggled nervously and kept waving her
wand, but nothing happened. I just glared at her.
I was NOT impressed!

Then, out of sheer frustration, Brianna angrily whacked her wand on the floor and shouted . . .

Her wand broke, and the star launched into the air like a guided missile!

Unfortunately, my FACE was in the wrong place at the wrong time. AGAIN! . . .

WHAM!!

I only have a vague memory of what happened after that. . . .

Brianna's magic spell didn't work! But that little
mishap with her broken wand DID!! . . .

594

WAKING UP AGAIN!!

"Look, everyone! I think she's finally coming to!" said a girl who sounded a lot like ~~Zoey~~ Red Riding Hood.

"Thank goodness!" said another girl, who sounded like ~~Chloe~~ Goldilocks. "At least she's not in a coma!"

"Um . . . is she supposed to be twitching like that?" asked a girl who sounded like the Wicked Witch of the West. "She looks like that dying roach I saw in the shower in the girls' locker room! I don't know which one is more DISGUSTING!"

"SHUT UP, MacKenzie!" both girls said in unison.

"You're the one who did this to her!"

"Yeah! You could have killed her!"

I slowly opened my eyes and squinted at the slightly blurry circle of faces staring down at me. . . .

And suddenly I started freaking out! "NO! Not the WICKED WITCH! HEEELLP!!" I screamed deliriously.

"RATS!! There are RATS in the DUNGEON!! The Queen of Hearts is going to chop off my HEAD!"

My arms flailed about as I imagined a hailstorm of dodgeballs slamming into my face. "THE BALLS! Please make the BALLS go away!"

"Nikki! Please calm down!" Chloe pleaded. She held up two fingers in front of my face. "Just try to focus, okay? How many fingers am I holding up?"

"Fingers? Those look like bunny ears to me," I muttered, staring at her blurry hand.

"You poor thing!" Zoey said, squeezing my arm. "You must be traumatized! But don't worry. You're going to be just fine. Trust me. Now close your eyes, relax, and take deep breaths, okay?"

"Where am I?" I asked groggily. "Where are the Munchkins? Am I still in Fairy Tale Land? Will someone please tell the room to stop spinning?"

That's when Chloe suddenly lost it.

"Fairy Tale Land?! Munchkins?! Nikki, snap out of it!" she yelled hysterically as she grabbed my shoulders and shook me as hard as she could. "I want my old friend back without the brain damage!"

"Stop it, Chloe!" Zoey scolded her. "If you keep shaking the poor girl like she's a Magic 8 Ball, she WILL be brain damaged!"

"Oops! Sorry about that!" Chloe apologized.

"Nikki is still a little disoriented," my gym teacher explained. "But luckily she doesn't appear to have any broken bones. Maybe she'll feel better if we get her up on her feet."

Chloe and Zoey each grabbed an arm and helped me stand up.

"Thanks, guys! I don't know what I'd do without you!" I said, starting to tear up.

"Nikki, we don't know what WE'D do without YOU!" Chloe sniffed.

598

"Yeah! We were SO scared when you got hurt!" Zoey said, dabbing at a tear.

Then they both gave me a bear hug and gushed . . .

"WE LOVE YOU, NIKK!!!
YOU'RE THE BEST BFF EVER!!"

After a few minutes the dizziness finally went away and I started to feel a lot better.

But get this!

I'd just had the CRAZIEST dream EVER!

About fairy tales!

It seemed SO real! I couldn't help but notice someone staring at me and nervously twirling her hair around her finger. . . .

It was MACKENZIE ☹!!

"OMG, Nikki! I'm so happy you're okay!" she said, plastering a fake smile across her face. "I was SUPERworried about you. It was so scary how you just ran into that ball after it slipped out of my hands! It was such a freak accident!"

The entire class and I just glared at that girl. She was such a liar.

"WHAT?! I didn't do anything w-wrong!" MacKenzie stammered. "I barely touched you!"

"I believe your last words were 'Hey, Maxwell! Eat this!'" Zoey quipped. "Sound familiar?"

"Just shut up and mind your own business!" MacKenzie spat. "I don't have to answer to YOU!"

"But you DO have to answer to Principal Winston," my gym teacher lectured sternly. "I saw everything, and, Miss Hollister, your behavior was totally UNACCEPTABLE! I'm sending you to the office so you can explain your actions to the principal."

"NO! You CAN'T send me to the office!!" MacKenzie shrieked. "It could end up on my permanent record! I'll be ruined! It's NOT fair! I'm going to tell my dad and . . ."

TWEEEEEEEEEET!!

When the gym teacher blew her whistle, MacKenzie
finally shut up and stopped ranting.

"Young lady, you can go to the office right NOW!
Or you can do it AFTER you run fifty laps around
this gym! It's YOUR choice!"

MacKenzie's face grew red with anger.

"Maxwell! You're a total . . . DORK!" she said
under her breath as she stormed out of the gym.

"MacKenzie, you say that like it's a BAD thing!"
I shot back. "But PLEASE! Don't HATE ME
because I'm DORKALICIOUS!"

"She totally deserves detention!" Zoey growled.

"For the rest of the YEAR!" Chloe snarled.

Then my gym teacher called my parents and
explained what had happened and told them that
I seemed to be okay.

Everyone agreed that it would be a good idea for me to visit the school nurse just for observation.

Actually, I didn't mind.

After everything I'd just been through, the thought of chillaxing on a comfy cot in the nurse's office with my diary sounded really good.

After we got dressed, Chloe and Zoey walked me to my locker.

Then we headed for the nurse's office.

That's when someone came running down the hall, yelling my name.

"NIKKI! NIKKI! I just heard what happened . . . !"

It was ~~Prince~~ Brandon!

He grabbed both of my hands and gazed into my eyes. . . .

SQUEEE!

"NIKKI! I WAS REALLY WORRIED!
ARE YOU OKAY?!"

OMG! It was total déjà vu! Almost like we had shared another life together!

"Actually, Brandon, I'm doing fine. But thank you for asking!" I giggled.

Brandon is such a nice guy! His reaction to the whole thing about me getting hurt in gym was just so . . . SWEET! And ROMANTIC!

SQUEEEEE ☺!!! Chloe and Zoey were practically melting into two syrupy puddles of gushiness!

Of course, MacKenzie had an attitude about the whole thing. I don't know why she is so jealous of my friendship with Brandon.

Anyway, after school everyone was gossiping about how Principal Winston gave MacKenzie a three-day detention for "unsportsmanlike behavior." And as part of detention, students help beautify our school. Of course, no place needed beautification more than the girls' showers!! . . .

MACKENZIE, SCRUBBING THE
GIRLS' SHOWERS DURING DETENTION!!

Even though I didn't appreciate that nasty little comment she made about me in gym, she was correct about there being roaches in the girls' showers.

EWW!!! That had to be the dirtiest job EVER!

I actually felt really sorry for her ☹!

NOT ☺!!

That girl has mercilessly teased and ridiculed me the ENTIRE school year because of my family's business.

But judging by the number of bugs I saw crawling on her, it looks to me like she might need to give Maxwell's Bug Extermination a call!

I'm just sayin' . . .

☺!!

BACK HOME! FINALLY ☺!! —4:15 p.m.

After my fairy tale FIASCO, I was mentally and physically exhausted.

I actually had to guzzle a soda just to get up enough energy to walk home from the bus stop. Otherwise, I probably would have collapsed and fallen asleep right there on Mrs. Wallabanger's front lawn.

OMG! I was SO happy to have finally made it HOME! I guess I've been taking it for granted for most of my life.

The very first thing I noticed was my ~~missing~~ stolen alarm clock sitting on the kitchen table!

And next to it was a sandwich and a note with MY name on it.

I also spotted a pair of ponytails with pink plastic flower barrettes peeking out from around the corner. . . .

ME, VERY HAPPY AND RELIEVED
TO FINALLY BE BACK HOME ☺!!

For some reason, everything at home seemed different.

Somehow . . . BETTER!

I couldn't wait to get back to my own room and sleep in my own bed.

I was even looking forward to seeing Mom and Dad. I planned on giving them both a really big hug just because I could.

And although I had been DREADING writing my own fairy tale, my head was now filled with so many exciting details from my OWN adventures that I thought it was going to BURST!

OMG! I had enough material to write a book. No! A book SERIES!

That assignment was going to be an easy A!

Anyway, I opened the letter with my name on it and immediately recognized Brianna's sloppy handwriting in purple crayon. . . .

ME, READING BRIANNA'S LETTER

This is what the letter said. . . .

Dear Nikki,

Try it! You might like it ☺!!

I wrote this letter to tell you that I am very, very sorry. When you are mad at me, your face looks like Daddy's when he smelled that skunk that was hiding in the garage. And this made me very sad. Your face, not the smelly skunk.

Are you still mad? Pleeze circle one: YES NO

If you are still mad, pleeze accept my sorryness for taking your clock, calling you a sandwich stealer, playing games on your phone and drawing my very cute face on it, and trying to call ~~Prise~~ Princess Sugar Plum.

I did not reech her. But I did reech a guy

named Moe by mistake, and he was not very polite at all. He said if I reech him again he will call the cops.

That would be very bad becuz I do not think they serve chicken nuggets in jail.

Then I would starve to death, which would not be a very fun time ☹.

Anyway, I made this sandwich just for you because I really care about you. I hope you love it!

You are my very best friend! After Miss Penelope and Princess Sugar Plum.

But you are the BESTEST sister I got ☺!!

Luv,
Brianna

OMG! Who would have thought an apology letter could tug at your heartstrings, bring tears to your eyes, AND make you laugh? ALL at the same time?

It was just SO . . .

Brianna!

That's when I decided to finally give in and try her stupid sandwich.

Especially since she had gone to the trouble to make it for me.

Just a tiny nibble probably wouldn't kill me. RIGHT?!

I closed my eyes and tried to pick up the squishy, gooey sandwich without totally freaking out.

But when I raised it to my mouth, the weird smell of pickles and peanut butter triggered my gag reflex!

 ICK ☹!!

"Don't think about it. Just EAT it!" I said to myself as I did a countdown.

"Five . . . four . . . three . . . two . . ." Nervous sweat trickled down my forehead. "ONE!"

I took a big bite and swallowed it as quickly as possible.

"OMG!" I moaned. I could NOT believe what my taste buds were screaming at me!

That sandwich was DELICIOUS!!

I took another bite. And then another!

How was it humanly possible to get all those amazing flavors into one sandwich?! It was the best sandwich I've ever had in my LIFE!

Brianna was still peeking at me from the doorway.

"Brianna! Come here! NOW!" I yelled with my mouth still full.

She timidly poked her head into the kitchen. "Who, me?"

"Yes, YOU!" I answered.

She walked up to me, folded her arms, and stared at her feet nervously.

That's when I gave her a huge hug.

I guess it took her by surprise, because she just stared at me and blinked like I was a two-headed monster or something.

"You're the BESTEST sister I got!" I giggled. "And this is the BESTEST sandwich ever!"

"Told you so!" Brianna grinned.

I had to admit, she was right!

"Okay, Brianna!" I said.

"I will eat it with a DOG!
I will eat it with a FROG!

I will eat it with a CAT!
I will eat it with a RAT!

I will eat it in my ROOM.
On the BUS. And on the MOON!

I will eat it NORTH and SOUTH!
It tastes so yummy in my MOUTH!

Call me PICKY! Call me FICKLE!
I so LOVE PBJ and PICKLES!!"

I fight with Brianna because sometimes she can be a spoiled BRAT!

But after today I'm actually starting to appreciate her good qualities. She's clever, cute as a button, friendly, creative, and she has a big heart.

But, most important, she's ALWAYS there for me when I need her!

As a big sister, I'd say I'm pretty lucky!

And one thing is for sure: Brianna is a WHOLE LOT better at making sandwiches than she ever was at being a fairy godmother. I'm just saying. . . .

ME AND BRIANNA,
SHARING HER YUMMY-LICIOUS SANDWICH ☺!!

Anyway, it's been THE craziest day EVER.

But the good news is that I ended up with my happily ever after!

Thanks to Brianna and all the people who really care about me ☺!

But I swear! If I get WHACKED in the face ONE more time, I'm going to totally lose it!!

Just kidding!

NOT!!!

I know . . . ! I know . . . !

I'm SUCH a DORK!!

☺!!

Rachel Renée Russell is the #1

New York Times bestselling author of the blockbuster book series Dork Diaries and the bestselling new series The Misadventures of Max Crumbly.

There are thirty million copies of her books in print worldwide, and they have been translated into thirty-seven languages.

She enjoys working with her two daughters, Erin and Nikki, who help write and illustrate her books.

Rachel's message is "Always let your inner dork shine through!"